THE NOVELS OF REX WARNER

The Novels of Rex Warner

An Introduction

N.H. Reeve
Lecturer in English
University College, Swansea

St. Martin's Press   New York

First published in the United States of America in 1989

Printed in Great Britain

Library of Congress Cataloging-in-Publication Data

Reeve, N. H., 1953—
The Novels of Rex Warner: An Introduction/ N.H. Reeve.
p. cm.
Includes bibliographical references.
ISBN 0–312–03703–1
1. Warner, Rex, 1905– — Criticism and interpretation.
I. Title
PR6045.A78Z88   1989
823'.912—dc20   89–37890
                                                          CIP

Contents

Acknowledgements

I should particularly like to thank the following for their varied and always generous help: Frances Arnold, Michael Bott and the University Library at Reading, George Butterick and the Homer Babbidge Library at Storrs, Connecticut, Sam Dawson, Richard Johnstone, Marion Lomax, Valerie Minogue, Jeremy Prynne, Arnold Rattenbury, Steven Tabachnick, John Turner, Rhys Williams, and especially Richard Kerridge.

N. H. Reeve

1

Introduction

Rex Warner (1905–86), whose writings deserve to be rescued from neglect, had a literary career in outline very similar to those of his better-known contemporaries. His education begins at a minor public school (St George's, Harpenden) and is completed at Oxford in the mid-1920s; he becomes friendly there with Auden, shares many of his interests, and is subsequently regarded as a kind of associate member of the 'Auden group'. He travels, teaches in various schools (being sacked from one, The Oratory School at Caversham, for political activity), and develops his rather unstable left-wing enthusiasms, which begin to subside as the 1930s draw to a close. His works are for a time keenly awaited and quite widely read,[1] and their public profile helps in his eventual enlistment as a more trustworthy Establishment figure; he moves from eager Communist (who sold the manuscript of his first novel to raise Party funds), to Director of the British Institute in Athens, within the space of a few years. After the war he concentrates on a second career as a teacher and translator of the classics, and while his original writing continues to discuss political and moral issues, its occasions become increasingly withdrawn from modern life, with the consequent loss of most of the vitality and excursiveness of his earlier work. Religious enquiry and faith meanwhile become steadily more important to him. Such a story, with relatively minor variations, could be told of a number of his fellows – Isherwood, Day Lewis, even Auden himself.

Yet the writings Warner produced are quite distinctive and personal. They may for convenience be called novels, but there is little danger of mistaking them for anyone else's. While the images and themes he works with reflect common preoccupations among his peers – frontiers, leadership, human and technological values – he developed his own literary forms for them, committing himself from the beginning not to the methods of orthodox realism but to prose allegory. He was not, except in a few relatively unsuccessful passages of his first book, *The Wild Goose Chase*, concerned to be at all stylistically innovative; he rather sought almost to excess a

1

clarity and plainness for his writing which would enable it to address basic themes directly and without ornament. In this respect his work aligns itself with the puritan allegorical tradition reaching back to Bunyan, rather than with the principal developments of literary modernism. His classical training led him additionally to aim for a detached, orderly, Lucretian overview, even while he implicitly questioned its tenability. All his writings express a concern for proportion and symmetry, for the values of the general over those of the exceptional, and for the kind of rhetorical crystallisation of what might be aspired to, rather than the exact recording of what was, whose use Thucydides first encouraged. Warner tried to organise the clutter and urgency of contemporary life into shapes whose form could be grasped and followed with some security; he wanted to enlighten his readers about abstract questions without removing them too far from the local and immediate. Hence his novels approach the ideas that interest him head-on, through strong set speeches about them, and obliquely, through the invention of symbolic occasions for meeting their unacknowledged presences in people's lives. His main characters are not merely stock allegorical types, or mouthpieces for the competing positions in the contemporary debate, but individuals whose experiences, consistently presented in relation to the influence on them of larger forces than themselves, could stand without complete loss of particularity for those of the many. At the same time the more powerful and interesting of the works involve a straining against or calling to account of the smoothly interlocking patterns on which they rely; there is a rebelliousness in them, which rarely interrupts the authoritative evenness of the writing, but which can work itself more insidiously into the texture.

   His literary output divides neatly in two. The main work is the sequence, published between 1937 and 1949, of five political allegories or novels-of-ideas, all subtitled in ways which draw attention to their non-realistic elements: *The Wild Goose Chase* (originally called 'an allegory', but in some editions 'a novel'), *The Professor* ('a forecast'), *The Aerodrome* ('a love story'), *Why Was I Killed?* ('a dramatic dialogue'), and *Men of Stones* ('a melodrama'); together with *Poems and Contradictions* of 1945, and a collection of essays, *The Cult of Power*, a year later. The second, less successful flowering, comprises four historical novels appearing between 1958 and 1967: *The Young Caesar*, *Imperial Caesar*, *Pericles the*

Athenian and *The Converts*. This essay takes the form of a commentary on the novels in chronological order. Its aim is simply to suggest something of what these works can yield to reading. It is not primarily concerned to rival the numerous excellent general studies of Warner's period which have secured his minor niche in literary history – for example Samuel Hynes's *The Auden Generation*, Richard Johnstone's *The Will to Believe*, or Katharine Hoskins's *Today the Struggle* – to all of which the present essay is indebted. Its particular enquiry is rather into the relationship between what Warner set out to say, and the forms in which he chose to say it. The main drift of the former has never been in much doubt, but some of the consequences of its interaction with the latter can provoke further interests than those Warner's name is usually associated with. Since only two of the novels, *The Professor* and *The Aerodrome*, are currently (1989) in print, a fair quantity of introductory exposition is involved, but I hope this will help to draw attention to the texts of works whose didactic intentions are usually regarded as sufficiently obvious for the details of their writing to be neglected. I believe that many of the questions raised both by the successes and the limitations of Warner's works continue to have considerable relevance, even in times ostensibly ready to dismiss both works and questions (an *Observer* reviewer in 1987 even coined the adjective 'Rex Warnerish', apparently to denote something recognisably puerile, turgid and pretentious); the possibilities of non-realistic or parabolic prose fictions not dissimilar to his own, as vehicles for diagnostic exploration of the contemporary world, are perhaps more widely courted now than in the 1950s and early 1960s when the reaction against the literary preoccupations of the 1930s was at its strongest. There are occasions when the very simplicity of Warner's methods can help to concentrate the attention upon some of the political, moral and aesthetic issues perennially involved in such writing. In *The Professor* (1938), for example, Warner does not just write a novel in order to discuss some of the problems of liberalism. He seeks to enact those problems in the structure of the fiction, and by so doing produces something richer and less clear-cut than the propaganda it initially looked like being; the implications of the fiction can simultaneously support and conflict with the message it is supposed to deliver. In *The Aerodrome* (1941), the sheer symmetry and comprehensiveness of the allegorical linkages stand in ambiguous relation with the welcome the novel affords to the uncertain and the unpredictable. Tensions of this kind are involved in each of Warner's fictional projects, and in sequence the works present a continuous reappraisal or modification of the positions their predecessors had reached. Proust wrote of Hugo that having begun by giving his readers thought, he proceeded to give them what was much more stimulating, food for thought; in Warner's case, an abundant and readily-digested supply of the former has perhaps obscured the presence of the latter, in works which have more than merely antiquarian or journalistic attractions.

The openings of Warner's novels can take a swift and arresting grip on their reader. Some involve an abrupt propulsion into a world that calls instantly for new bearings, while we hear as it were the clanging-shut of the gates behind us:

> I continually wonder how I may account for my present state, which, I suppose, it would be accurate to describe as one of death.
>
> (*Why Was I Killed?*)

> The last week enjoyed, or rather experienced, by Professor A. may be reconstructed with tolerable accuracy from two sources . . .
>
> (*The Professor*)

Elsewhere there are breathless plunges – anxiously reined back by qualifying asides or meticulous punctuation – into a kind of vertigo:

> It seems, though it was many years ago, only yesterday that we citizens of a seaside town, standing in ranks along the esplanade, watched, cheering at the same time with all the force of our lungs, the outset of the three brothers who, with the inconsiderate fine daring of youth, were prepared, each in his own way, to go far on bicycles, distinguishing our town by an attempt which even the brothers only dimly understood and which seemed to most of us who stood spectators vociferously cheering impracticable, to some even ridiculous.
>
> (*The Wild Goose Chase*)

> It would be difficult to overestimate the importance to me of the events which had taken place previous to the hour (it was

shortly after ten o'clock in the evening) when I was lying in the marsh near the small pond at the bottom of Gurney's meadow, my face in the mud and the black mud beginning to ooze through the spaces between the fingers of my outstretched hands, drunk, but not blindly so, for I seemed only to have lost the use of my limbs.

(*The Aerodrome*)

In their various ways these openings register a shock or instability from which the rest of the novel will be an attempt to recover. They are variants of the traditional entry into allegory, seeking to concentrate a whole span of time and experience into a single gesture of dislocation; in such cases the specific occasions may be bizarre, but the moods they evoke can be more generally recognised. If recovery is to take place, it will be by way of a patient journey towards the meaning of what in its initial impact was unaccountable; hence the fall into allegory is one which simultaneously isolates the individual subject and creates around him a community of understanding, to which his experience mutely appeals. Dante's dark wood is his own, but the erosion of the customs on which identity and order were constructed, the loss of the way and the falling into sleep, have an unlimited constituency. In the case of Warner's generation, born into the securities of an Edwardian middle-class childhood and ejected from it by the consequences of a world war they were too young to take part in, the breach between what had been expected and what was found had perhaps a particular sharpness; a sense of the fraudulence of what they had been led to believe consorted with a guilty awareness of having survived disturbances which cost their elder brothers everything. In such conditions the transition from one state of life to the next can no longer be smooth and direct; as Rod Mengham argued à propos Edward Upward's *The Railway Accident*, the individual subject is now 'forced to participate in the world through a chain of actions it would never freely choose'.[2] Since the past has voluntarily absconded along with its promise, one's freedom to reject it and start afresh has also been curtailed; the experience of cutting or being cut loose, which actuates movement in *The Wild Goose Chase* and *The Aerodrome*, is then less one's liberation from a fixed and stifling pattern which threatened one's independence, than itself an element of the fate in whose grip one continues to struggle.

The literature of the time finds various ways of registering the anxieties of this transition, either by discussing it directly or by allowing the upheavals to surface in form and language. Warner's allegories typically do both. They tend always to involve the conflicts of will and determinism, since they trace the desire to be folded once again, as in the days before the breach, in the embrace of an order, without becoming so perfectly absorbed in it that the spirit of revolt is finally suffocated. In pursuit of an accommodation of the two, the forms of narrative allegory which he uses offer alternatives to the apparent meanings of what is found in the world, without permitting those alternatives to proliferate indefinitely. They seek to recover a measure of control, whereby the individual finds reassurance that his actions do have significance even in a world whose immediate complications seem overwhelming; they seek to disclose the basic structure on which those complications rest, in order to simplify one's practical relations with them. Samuel Hynes took up Auden's loose term 'parable' to locate the characteristics of much writing from Warner's period: 'clarifying, instructive . . . it renders the feeling of human issues . . . it offers models of the problem of action'.[3] The parable was typically a means of channelling, into something more open and generous, the youthful urge to preach and castigate one's way out of distress, and, however naively, to keep connected to the public arena experiences which might easily have been dissipated in isolated grumblings. The more formal procedures of allegory which Warner adopts register in addition that first disturbance, that Fall whereby the subject becomes aware of a difference or gap between his former perceptions and the new state, along with the circuitous route to such security as will redeem him from his initial giddiness.

In *The Wild Goose Chase* and *The Professor* the security is ostensibly recovered by the steady application of rational socialist principles. The restabilising efforts of allegory are here aligned with a political awakening. But the optimism of those early ambitions for the allegorical method, that it should rescue the child's source of comfort without forfeiting the adult's critical detachment from it, finds itself increasingly at odds with a pathos and fragility perhaps similar, if not issuing in a comparable passion, to that which Gulliver found at the end of his private quest for the orderly and undivided State. Swift is able to present both the astonished fascination and the nightmare of the country of the Houyhnhnms from the perspective of one who had been 'a Sort of Projector in my younger Days',[4] the mind clinging on to the hopes which its workings are exposing. Warner, without having at his command a style that could establish and twine itself around so many complexities, traces through his novels a like ambivalence rooted in his work from its beginnings.

Warner went up to Wadham College in 1923 with a classical scholarship. Conventional expectations of him were more than fulfilled by his early successes; his tutor Maurice Bowra found him 'the ideal pupil, since he had been badly grounded at school and found in Greek and Latin all the charms of novelty',[5] and Warner proceeded to gain 13 Alphas in his 15 Mods papers. His achievements in combining academic triumph with outstanding success as a rugby player proved powerful attractions to the young Auden; there is a passing tribute to Warner's brilliance as a wing three-quarter in *Paid on Both Sides*. (One recollection Warner always cherished was having once been described, by a rugby correspondent assessing team selection for a local newspaper, as 'the most dangerous man in the South-West of England'). But while gregarious and fond of undergraduate literariness, he seems occasionally to have reacted against the lionising and coterie tendencies in which he was expected to figure. Day Lewis, his closest friend from those times, recalled Warner's predilection (not, in his case, sexually motivated) for 'raffish bar-room types',[6] and in *The Aerodrome* Warner shows his hero, Roy, maintaining an awkward balance between condescension and real friendship with his rustic drinking companions. Warner was also given to occasional maverick gestures, blacklegging during the General Strike, for example, despite his professed left-wing sympathies (he conducted a tram in Hull), and rationalising his enjoyment with the view that, since the government would inevitably defeat the strikers, they should be helped to do so as quickly as possible. The immediate impression produced is not so much of a particularly complex personality as of one anxious not to be too simply categorised. Certainly he seems to have combined an uneasiness or diffidence about his talents and inclinations with an exuberant pleasure in the moments when they afforded him mastery of a situation. In *The Aerodrome* again he has Roy reflect, in such familiar and unassuming terms as hold so many keys to aesthetic and emotional delight, upon the 'confidence and exhilaration' which accrue from being able suddenly to seize control amid 'the surprising and the accidental':

At the moments of taking-off and of landing I had felt much the
same feeling as a footballer has from time to time, when he sees
instantaneously a gap in the defence and his own ability to break
through it.

(The Aerodrome, p. 189)

Intellectually, however, he came at this time close to a dangerous
overloading. A feverish rush at the systems of philosophy brought
on what used to be called a 'nervous breakdown'. It was clearly
serious enough to inspire the kind of wryly embroidered anecdotes
that make such things safely memorable and humorous; Day Lewis
wrote that Warner 'saw the Absolute walk in at his door',[7] Bowra
that 'he was said to see the transcendental deduction of the categories lying in solid blocks across the room'.[8] It certainly marked
the end of any immediate academic aspirations Warner may have
had, and when he returned to Oxford after a year's absence it was
to take things easy, gain a Pass degree in English, and proceed, as
did most of his literary companions, to a career as a schoolmaster.

He made his first mark, at Oxford and after, as a poet. Indeed,
although he was experimenting intermittently with various ideas
which eventually became by 1932–33 substantially *The Wild Goose
Chase*, he did not actually publish any prose fiction until his boy's
adventure-story, *The Kite*, appeared in 1936. His poetic work,
collected later in *Poems* (1937) and *Poems and Contradictions* (1945),
has its attractiveness, but is often too heavily derivative, especially
from Hopkins, of whom Warner was one of the earliest imitators.
The sonnet sequence entitled *Contradictions*, obscurely charting the
collapse of a love affair in terms of an evolutionary process of
which individual attachments are only symptoms, conveys a
struggle for supremacy between growth and settlement, or between political and aesthetic concerns, of a similar nature to those
generally conducted in a less self-conscious and rhetorically explicit manner in the prose works. The poems only occasionally
achieve sufficient sureness of touch to make the ground on either
side of this struggle firmly defensible. There is much sprung
rhythm, or something like it, and much use of the aggressive starts
of medieval alliteration, but too often these appear as the components of a serviceable technique, imposed upon the subject rather
than registering a genuinely vigorous response to its pressures.
One early sonnet, discussed by A. T. Tolley in *The Poetry of the
Thirties* (London 1975, p.146), exemplifies the strengths and

limitations of much of the work. The poet as crusader of Necessity criticises his weaker self:

> How sweet only to delight in lambs and laugh by streams,
> innocent in love wakening to the early thrush,
> to be awed by mountains, and feel the stars friendly,
> to be a farmer's boy, to be far from battle.
> But me my blood binds to remember men more than the
> birds ...
> ... How should I live then but as a kind of fungus,
> or else as one in strict training for desperate war?

The unspoken recognition of the poem is of the mutual dependence of these two selves; the crude energies which heap up violent and glamorous declamation arise from guilt about the readiness with which the poem's real desires can be written down to a kind of dreamful ease. The admonishment which regards the nature-lover as a parasitical growth unless he takes up arms seems itself rather too easy. Similar choices offered in answer to the key question in Warner, 'how should I live?', are considered more effectively in *The Professor*; the opening quatrain of this poem has a fresh lilt and grace that survives the subsequent weight of anxiety simply by being unequal to it.

Several other poems, including good lines and images, are about the birds this poem claims to want to forget. Birds, flight and associated imagery and symbolism recur frequently throughout Warner's fiction. He himself hated flying, and during his years as a classicist in America always preferred to cross the Atlantic by ship, even at considerable personal inconvenience, but he was a passionate enthusiast of bird-watching. The first paragraph of *The Kite* has its boy-hero casually doing just that:

> 'Hullo! That must be a kite,' John said to himself ... What marvellous birds they were! How they seemed to finger the currents of air with their feathers! With what easy mastery they turned and dived and hovered, all the time mewing up in the blue like unearthly cats! Yet here, close to the ground, and, as it were, out of their element, how cumbrous and shabby they appeared. There was even something repulsive in the gestures of their snaky necks as they eyed everything on earth with suspicion.
>
> (*The Kite*, p. 5)

The simple contrast drawn here, between glittering distant free-dom and carrion-eating meanness close-to, is applied to drug trafficking in the Middle East. *The Kite* is a boy's thriller, written at the behest of Day Lewis's friend L. A. G. Strong, who edited a Blackwell's series, 'Tales of Action by Men of Letters'. Warner's is a competently crafted attempt to combine the usual conventions with a socially-progressive theme. It is set in Egypt and Cyprus, where Warner had worked and travelled in his twenties; the strangeness, to a well-brought-up English boy like John, of the landscapes and customs, is effectively evoked. The story is well packed with kidnapping, code-breaking, escapes, car chases, and a series of mysterious baroque murders. Warner makes particular use of two familiar ingredients of the genre, the uncle and the secret society. The uncle is characteristically the source of the adventure, allowing the child a controlled release from the restric-tions laid on him by parents and school; he introduces a new approach to experience without disposing entirely of the ground-rules to which the child is ultimately bound to return. This particular Uncle Frank is a wise colonial hand, who offers his nephew a salty knowledge of the world and of the relative place, for good and ill, that the English occupy in it. Their relationship permits a mutual affection without a full commitment, thus easing many of the pangs of adolescent self-consciousness; it is quite without the homosexual and autogenitive overtones that surround the uncle-figure in Auden's *The Orators*, for example. As for the secret society, John is caught up with a band of youthful Egyptian socialists, who are fighting to free their country from the drug trade, which is seen as an inevitable consequence of colonial exploitation and local impoverishment. The discovery and defeat of the smuggling boss known as 'The Kite' is regarded as an essential prerequisite of any orderly transition towards future autonomy and responsible government in Egypt. Instead of offer-ing a general hostility towards England as the principal imperialist power, which might have been expected, these youngsters are concerned to discriminate between 'good' foreigners, like John's uncle, steeped in the culture of the host country, and bad ones, who merely take advantage of its weaknesses. Warner manages to convey several sweetened doses of instruction – about racial prejudice, about the political conditions underlying apparently random abuses, about the size of the world beyond Dover cliff – without talking down to his readers, and without ever suggesting that such problems could seriously threaten or overwhelm a steadily applied rational intelligence, such as John and Frank jointly possess. Their mixture of innate English resourcefulness and gradually broadening understanding in the face of temptations to isolate and mystify makes some aspects of *The Kite* a dummy run for *The Wild Goose Chase*; the latter draws numerous effects from the traditions of children's literature. Meanwhile the ubiquitous presence of the eponymous bird, discrediting its own romantic attractiveness every time it comes close enough to be properly seen, is a constant reminder of the various illusions and false enchantments of adolescence or the unthinking shelter of home. Here such things can be dismantled without any problematic regret, since the sheer numbers and familiarity of the kites make them quickly wearisome. Hence the boy-hero John, who never lingers over his impressions, is rather priggish and superior, keen to play his part in the progressive alliance of English decency and Egyptian democratic socialism towards the greater good his uncle describes: 'If people are permitted to make easy money out of doing harm, harm will be done . . . it's much more difficult to . . . suppress those conditions which make the laws necessary' (pp. 190–1). No doubt all boys who use their fortuitous adventures as sticks to measure the opinions and prejudices of those not yet embarked on one are priggish – this one at least in a good cause.

In 1937 Warner reached the attention of a larger public when Boriswood finally published *The Wild Goose Chase*, largely through the good offices of John Lehmann. *The Wild Goose Chase* is a long, sprawling, vigorous allegory, whose hero, George, embarks on an unending pursuit of the Wild Goose, 'a symbol of our Saviour', as the prefatory poem claims; it represents freedom, vitality, love, whatever conduces to fulfilled and unrepressed life. George travels through a fantasy land of frustration and sterility, ruled by a tyrannical city which is eventually overthrown by revolution, but even after this triumph the Wild Goose, though nearer, is not finally tracked to its lair. Lehmann was attracted by what he saw as the book's exploration of current preoccupations, political and moral, predominantly in the field of action rather than of individual psychology.[9] This made it a neat companion for another novel in whose progress Lehmann took an active interest, Edward Upward's *Journey to the Border*, which emphasised the hero's mental landscape. Warner's concentration on activity may well have seemed appropriate to the time of the outbreak of the Spanish

Civil War, where issues which were previously the subject of much
agonised wrangling appeared at last to have been joined and
simplified. Certainly the publication of the novel coincided with
the peak of Warner's enthusiasm for communism, expressed
discursively in two essays he wrote around this time – 'Education',
for the collection *The Mind in Chains*, edited by Day Lewis in 1937,
and the pamphlet 'We're not going to do Nothing', attributed to
Day Lewis but largely written for him by Warner[10] in reply to
Aldous Huxley's pacifist appeal 'What are you going to do about
it?' in 1936. These essays present quite orthodox versions of the
views of those to whom socialism was essentially liberalism put
into action, the last development of romantic humanism and the
final clearance of the impasse liberalism had reached.

But *The Wild Goose Chase* itself has a mood a little different from
that of the rehearsed and glibly decisive arguments of the manifes-
toes. It has a discontentment and rebelliousness reaching back well
before the Spanish war, predating also, for the most part the rise of
Hitler and the effect of that development on political attitudes. The
uprising called for in the novel is still that of the workers against
iniquitous capitalism; the targets of the satire largely belong to a
world of late-1920s, early-1930s apathy and decadence, variously
allegorised as the suppression of vital forces by a loose conspiracy
of enemies. The hermaphrodite literati, the feeble-minded cabaret
singers, the solipsistic dons and the treacherous clergymen which
the hero, George, meets during his first exposure to the life of the
city, seem however distantly to conflate aspects of the young
Warner's own naive enthusiasms and first angry disappointments.
On occasions when such characters appear to have specific models,
they tend to derive from a period which, although not far off, is by
the publication date of 1937 already historical rather than strictly
contemporary. The figure of the First King, for example, practising
fencing in his office and calling for 'a modern aristocracy of Action
and of Genius' to 'usher in the new age' (*The Wild Goose Chase*,
p. 219), looks like a caricature of Oswald Mosley, but Mosley in the
period 1931–32, moving from the New Party towards the British
Union of Fascists; his influence had almost completely evaporated
by the time the novel appeared. Compared with the confident, if
misplaced, hauteur of the 1936–37 essays, *The Wild Goose Chase*
seems gauche and intemperate, wildly scattering its shot in the
direction of whatever happens to come into view, across the span
of a decade and its changes. This youthful strain is the source

of its peculiar combination of power and absurdity; it expresses satirical disgust towards pretensions it sees no reason to dignify with subtler treatment. The symptoms of the general malaise initially, and strikingly, appear to the young man to be jokes, so transparent that it is impossible to believe they could pose a serious threat, or that anyone could be deceived by them. The chagrin of his subsequently discovering the real grip they exert, the anger and exasperation that lashes out on recognising how such abuses rely upon a certain implicit collusion on the part of their victims, are impulses and emotions strongly hinted at underneath the writing even where they are not fully explored in it. The impression of scatter and range in the novel is reinforced by a number of incidental stylistic experiments and the variety of genres and conventions drawn upon, largely for comic effect. The apparent randomness is not, however, a sign of submission to the flux, but a series of digressions to emphasise the strong central plan of the quest-allegory, whose model is *The Pilgrim's Progress*. I attempt a fuller discussion of the novel, and of the mutual impact of method and matter, in the second chapter of this study. The coarseness in *The Wild Goose Chase* does not vitiate its more intelligent arguments and its deeper sympathies; it is easy to mock George's crude chauvinism and cartoon triumphs, as lissom girls and heroic peasants fall regularly at his feet, but even in his most committed writing Warner never believed that a socialist revolution would really cure everything – rather that it was a prerequisite of curing anything.

Warner retained an affection for his first novel and campaigned intermittently through the 1960s and 1970s for it to be rediscovered, without great success. He regarded it for all its faults as a more interesting work than *The Professor*, which was the only one of his novels to be considered at any length in Samuel Hynes's *The Auden Generation*, somewhat to Warner's disappointment. The omission of *The Wild Goose Chase* is rather curious, since its ingredients are so liberally distributed as to make it almost a pot-pourri of what Hynes elsewhere regarded as most typical and prominent in its period: the journey over the frontier to an imaginary country, the search for a leader to heal a sick society, the eagerness to break with the past, the allegorical test to distinguish weak and strong. So described, of course, these items fall into line a little too readily. But the catalogue misses both the satirical power and the flavour of the book, described by Monroe Spears as 'probably the best single work from which to recapture the intellectual and emotional atmosphere of the times'.[11]

For *The Professor*, which appeared in October 1938, the approach has substantially changed. In this novel Warner begins to find his characteristic style, which does not vary greatly thereafter. The prose is restrained, almost over-precise in its concern to be clear at each moment; the details of the world it shapes are suggested rather than filled in; it sketches instead careful outlines, bare and exposed in their simplicity. There is still an imaginary country with its allegorical figures and events, but there is little of the plenitude and glee of invention which kept *The Wild Goose Chase* going through its more arid or embarrassing stretches. The worlds presented in *The Professor* and the novels which succeed it are concentrated to their most urgent essentials, standing in relief against a lightly-touched background. The contemporary occasions on which the allegory obliquely comments are also much fore-shortened: in this case, events loosely modelled on the annexation of Austria in March 1938 are compacted into seven days. Warner's subject in *The Professor* is very far from the freedom of unfledged youth to roam in search of fulfillment. He presents instead a nightmare of liberalism, forced to collude in its own overthrow by its inability to muster a defence. The new Chancellor of a small European state, a middle-aged Professor of Classics, who sounds at times like a reminiscence of Gilbert Murray, vainly seeks to uphold the liberal virtues during a crisis which his very anxiety to be tolerant and responsible prevents him from understanding. His beliefs are indicted by various opponents for having contributed to the impending calamity of fascist conquest, and the rapidity of the events in the novel (which Warner uses very effectively) snatches away the breathing-space liberalism traditionally relies on to consider the competing arguments. Socialism offers itself at the critical juncture as the only serious option for those to whom humane ideals are dear but currently corrupted and weaponless. But the socialist commitment undertaken by the younger genera-tion is presented in this novel without enthusiasm or joy. It is a kind of tragic necessity, a last desperate chance to make a meaning-ful resistance rather than a merely impotent gesture; it is thrown into ironic relation with the Greek tragic models the Professor is fond of quoting. The novel does open with the image of a notional future, in which the current pressure to suspend humane impulses in favour of ruthless necessary action will have relented. But this image is soon obscured by the onrush of the immediate terror. If a precarious flicker of light does remain, it does not just derive from the hope invested in the socialist critique of liberalism. In the course of the novel the Professor's own character, with its naive integrity and, eventually, its flexibility and openness to change, comes to carry with it an implicit challenge of its own, to some of the harsher presentments which the socialists – it is charitably suggested – have been obliged by the exigency of the times to make. When the Professor's son, a revolutionary leader, says of a discredited trade unionist 'perhaps he would be useful' (p. 247), we may catch an ominous glimpse of where collectivism might be heading, which this novel, driven by the instant requirement, cannot avoid seeing but has no time to pursue.

The Aerodrome, published in 1941 but written in the summer of 1939, does begin the pursuit, and in the process erases the last traces of Marxist faith to which *The Professor* had clung with edgy confidence. Warner's initial hopes for the communism currently practised had been – to put it no more harshly – over-sanguine. But he did see that the anxious impulses towards order and control, anxieties underlying even the most high-minded desires for social reconstruction, could easily issue in a fascist cult of which the organisations officially known to be fascist had no monopoly. The simplifications which ensue from what the Professor's son had called 'the dictatorship of an idea' (p. 88) are now considered in the light of attractions far removed from the idealistic fervour or intellectual conviction of the young radicals of the earlier novels; the principal concern of *The Aerodrome* is its narrator Roy's attempt to recover the psychological and emotional security which his perception of the hollowness of his world had cost him. The site of this quest is an unremarkable English village only momentarily disturbed by violence or drama, and the investigation is as much into the hidden entanglements of what had always been seen and taken for granted, as into the brave new world awaiting its moment to conquer. The old village world struggles with 'fumbling conventions' (p. 261) to cover its inadequacies; the new world's eager success in pointing these out temporarily screens its own shortcomings. Eventually these emerge, to reveal how the fascist vision is not an invitation to meet the grandeur of the world but to protect oneself from it. Roy wanders into fascism and out again for purely personal reasons, never showing any real interest in the detail of its wider aims and policies. It is the simple sense of having a purpose, rather than its nature, which supplies for him the twin needs whose relationship dominates Warner's allegories: adventurousness and a reassuring embrace. Roy eventually reaches a position of greater confidence in the face of the intricacy of things, but the novel, by revealing in the texture of its prose how much his new attitude owes to the creeds he claims to have rejected, continues to offer something more complex and disturbing than the satisfactory resolution its narrator imagines for himself.

The Aerodrome has always been the most popular and successful of Warner's books. By 1950 it had been translated into 11 languages. But despite periodic efforts to revive it, including a television adaptation, it remains puzzlingly neglected. It has a remoteness that risks occasional banality, but it registers most economically much that was of real significance to Warner's kind and generation, without being completely circumscribed by the earnestness of its intentions. It never quite finds a language that could render the particularities of its hero's experience more creatively, but by remaining at the level of mildly perturbed bemusement and tentativeness it leaves that experience open to a larger number of possible equivalents. The attempt, as in Warner's favourite classical models, is always to connect local detail with large abstract forces, with a language which jumps over the whole middle ground, the more routinely habitable area of liberal realism, which as always in Warner is indicated in passing rather than comprehensively explored.

Around this time the notion of Warner as an 'English Kafka' began to gain credence. So much so that in 1945 the first issue of a new literary magazine, *Focus*, devoted half its space to a symposium discussing the two authors and their supposed relationship. Warner himself had voiced a common view of the time by regarding the Kafka of *The Castle* and *The Trial* as having given allegorical expression to 'the pervasive sense of guilt which, known to us or unknown, marks the modern man in a world of war and insecurity, believing in his individuality, but all the time at the mercy of abstract forces, economic, political or psychological'.[12] This is the Kafka of the deferred or withheld meaning, of the unhappy collusion of the subject in his own defeat, which enabled him in some quarters to be regarded as the prophet of totalitarianism. (The personal and Judaic elements in Kafka's work, not to mention the wild humour of so much of it, tended to be overlooked.) One can see in Warner's remarks his finding in Kafka a model of his own preoccupations, which is perhaps a clearer statement of the relationship between the two writers than could emerge from the question of direct influence. In common with other members of Auden's circle, Warner had begun writing allegory well before translations of Kafka's works became widely available (the first, Muir's version of *The Castle*, appeared in England in 1930), and as Joyce Crick pointed out in an essay on 'Kafka and the Muirs', it was less that Kafka taught the English to write allegory than that they were already primed to read Kafka in allegorical terms.[13] Most of the contributors to the *Focus* symposium agree that the two authors' intentions in using allegorical techniques differ considerably; many of them, while bestowing some praise on *The Aerodrome*, tend to use Kafka as a stick to beat Warner with, unfavourably contrasting the latter's simplicity and concern to clarify the apparently obscure, with the former's 'pioneering' relation with 'hovering eternities' (Rajan), his 'new charting of the human situation' (Allen), his using an allegory which 'creates an experience whereas Warner's only reproduces' (Enright). (The anarchist George Woodcock put forward a dissenting view, determined even at the cost of a very partial reading to enlist Warner for the antiauthority cause; he regarded *The Aerodrome* as 'ultimately more satisfying than any [novel] of Kafka's', because its 'world of relationships is limited to that of humanity and its proximate, physical environment'. He at least implicitly raised the question of whether the indefinitely interpretable symbolism most of the other contributors found in Kafka was in all cases and necessarily of greater value than the efforts towards rebalancing and demystification in Warner's allegories.)[14]

Comparisons between English authors and Kafka tended to be seized upon by eager reviewers because Kafka's name was a talisman of all that was exciting and up-to-date. But much the more straightforward European influence on Warner's work was that of Dostoyevsky. Around the time of the *Focus* argument Warner produced a lengthy essay on 'Dostoyevsky and the Collapse of Liberalism'[15] which makes clear his indebtedness. Dostoyevsky's direct portrayal of conflicting creeds in argument and in action, and in particular his own ambivalent response, what Warner called his 'fascinated feelings of attraction to and repulsion from the ideals of the liberal and the revolutionary' (p. 44), seem, however retrospectively read by his essay into Warner's own work, the main sources of what is strong in it. So much so that from this point onwards in his career, his self-consciousness as to what he was doing tends to drain his fiction of much of its urgency. *Why Was I Killed?* (1943) tries to investigate the meaning of the war fought against the fascism whose origins Dostoyevsky had traced in the unrestrained rationalism of the liberal atheist; *Men of Stones* (1949) uses the Grand Inquisitor as the model for its central character, the Governor. Although new points of view and situations are introduced in these works, they are for the most part content to remain within the areas of interest traced in the first three novels; they include much trenchant commentary upon what has happened to those areas as a result of the Second World War, without finding new methods or techniques to respond to the changes they are acutely conscious of. In *Men of Stones* especially, the conflict between Warner's now-familiar approach, organising clashes among characters or situations which localise and embody general issues, and the resistance of the material he uses to being so abstracted, trails off in a kind of deadlock; the allegory of ideas, so explicitly reliant on Dostoyevskian sources, struggles to make headway in a context where ideas are held down by apocalyptic visions and have no room for manoeuvre.

Warner signed a contract with the Bodley Head in January 1950 to write three more novels, but nothing came of it; a further contract two years later was for three 'entertainment' novels, in the distinction made by Graham Greene, but only one of these was ever written. This was *Escapade*, which appeared in 1953. It is a rather clumsy and leaden-footed attempt to satirise the allegorical methods his readers were accustomed to; the stock characters of an Ealing comedy English village called Average are subjected to threats from poorly-disguised spies and secret agents. *Escapade*'s humour only intermittently hits the mark. Warner had produced several much more successful moments of comedy and satire in his earlier works, when he was writing less self-consciously and more in the heat. Here the evidence is too clear, of declining artistic engagement and loss of direction – a version of the predicament of the political prisoners pithily described in *Men of Stones*, who would, if released from their long captivity, 'automatically rally to their various banners, and yet they would be uneasily conscious that those banners had, in the meantime, been redesigned' (p. 13). The enthusiasms of the 1930s had become routinised and stunted by lack of clear achievement, while many of the writers who held them were caught up in the anxieties of their own retractions and the loss of what had at least appeared to be a public platform, with an audience created by the occasion. Warner wrote no more fiction in his former style, returning instead with historical novels closely based on his classical translations, of Caesar's *Gallic Wars*, Thucydides and Plutarch.

In these his interests in the problems of leadership and the idea of the great man are more expansively pursued. In *The Wild Goose Chase* leadership as practised by George was thought of as a temporary condition, adopted in an emergency and to be relinquished when communist conditions had been established; but since these still lay over the horizon the full issue of that intended abdication and its consequences was never joined. *The Professor* tried to argue that the qualities which liberalism admired in its leaders were of limited value without a supporting framework, of effective power and absolute conviction, which the liberal conscience, with its emphasis on private freedom and disinterested judgement, could never commit itself to. While liberalism was paralysed by its efforts to understand all sides, the dictators of *The Aerodrome* and *Men of Stones* sought a futile escape in reconstructing the human subject which had to abide the question. But Julius Caesar, as Warner presents him in his two 'autobiographical' novels, while no less paternalist and authoritarian, understands both the reality of the mass forces on which his powers depend, and of his own mortality, with the consequent need to construct a system of government which can endure independently of himself. Unlike the Professor he sees that speed of movement and seizure of opportunity irrespective of principle are the only routes to success; unlike the Air Vice-Marshal or the Governor he sees that the power he wields is greater than he is, and that the first priority must be to establish that authority as the natural and accepted state rather than to use it as an instrument for imposing abstract ideas on the world. Caesar's success is that of a pragmatism which is not at odds with recklessness and daring; it is the blending of what might conventionally be called 'leadership qualities' with what the particular times can conduce to and recognise as such. Warner's concern was always to locate such possibilities historically, rather than to claim they were freely available at any moment; he thus retains vestiges of his older Marxist thinking in the midst of a more conservative, even Hobbesian analysis. Caesar presents his own case, untouched by another's judgement; the shortcomings of his position emerge in the blindnesses of his own account of it. But this is not so for *Pericles the Athenian* or for St Augustine in *The Converts*; in these novels the heroes are not offered for the reader's rigorous inspection, but are idealised with humourless reverence by narrators who express Warner's now pallid nostalgia for grand simplicities which his own times cannot offer. While these last two books still contain a number of interesting and thoughtful meditations, they represent the final decline of Warner's creative powers, and he wisely refused the temptation to go on repeating himself. In the early 1970s a French cinema company expressed interest in filming a version of *Men of Stones*, but the project foundered in a morass of contractual difficulties, and Warner's literary career was effectively over.

His art was always essentially occasional, in that it required an external stimulus to react against; bereft of any sense of involvement in the contemporary world, he had turned to classical history for the raw material on which he could work, but he had too scrupulous a respect for it to allow himself much in the way of imaginative transformation. But the significance of his best work is not restricted to the stimulating occasion. It is always motivated, on however small a scale, by a heroic enthusiasm, to subject the complications of its material to an aesthetic order which can show those complications in a grander context than that of a merely personal reaction to them. But because that concern for finish, resolution, clarity, is worked against a background of uncertainty and contradiction, the very failure of Warner's art to carry off exactly the accomplishment it seeks can stand as a kind of moral rescue, an openness in spite of the will to closure, a tacit acknowledgement of limits, which does not pre-empt the urge to defy them but arises from the act of doing so. I trust that mine is not too perverse a hope, that his work may continue to be read not only for what it achieves, but for what it can intimate in falling short of achieving.

Notes

1. Anthony Burgess gives a typically anecdotal account of having been one of those 'thoughtful corporals' who read Rex Warner and other 'novelists of ideas' during the war, in the course of his Introduction to *The Aerodrome*, Oxford 1982, pp. 8–9.

2. Rod Mengham, 'Smithereens: *The Railway Accident* and *The Orators*', in *Ideas and Production* IV, 1985, p. 31.

3. Samuel Hynes, *The Auden Generation*, London 1976, p. 15.
4. *The Prose Works of Jonathan Swift*, vol. 11, Oxford 1941, p. 162.
5. Maurice Bowra, *Memories*, London 1966, p. 149.
6. C. Day Lewis, *The Buried Day*, London 1960, p. 220.
7. Day Lewis, p. 166.
8. Bowra, p. 149.
9. John Lehmann, *The Whispering Gallery*, London 1955, pp. 246–7.
10. Sean Day Lewis, *C. Day Lewis: An English Literary Life*, London 1980, p. 99.
11. Monroe K. Spears, *The Poetry of W. H. Auden: The Disenchanted Island*, New York and Oxford 1963, p. 83.
12. Rex Warner, 'The Uses of Allegory', in *Penguin New Writing* 17, 1943, p. 148.
13. Joyce Crick, 'Kafka and the Muirs', in *The World of Franz Kafka*, ed. J. P. Stern, London 1980, pp. 159–74.
14. *Focus One*, ed. Rajan and Pearse, Dennis Dobson, London 1945. References are to the essays by B. Rajan (p. 13), Walter Allen (p. 32), D. J. Enright (p. 38), and George Woodcock (p. 65).
15. Rex Warner, 'Dostoyevsky and the Collapse of Liberalism', in *The Cult of Power*, London 1946.

2

Allegory and *The Wild Goose Chase*

In his study *Reading the Thirties*, Bernard Bergonzi remarked of Warner's first novel, *The Wild Goose Chase*, that it 'moved from crude allegory to ... genuine symbolism ... and back again disconcertingly'.[1] This comment, while pointing to an intermittently productive tension in the text which need not be so cavalierly dismissed, speaks eloquently of the post-Romantic critical assumptions as to the relative status of allegory and symbol. A writer setting out in the late 1920s with a commitment to an allegorical method – and in Warner's case to a revival of the tradition of Protestant quest–narrative, where doubt journeys towards faith – is running deliberately aslant the contemporary literary tendencies. Insofar as the challenge of allegory at such a moment involves posing certainty against liberal indefiniteness, abstraction against naturalism, satirical outline against fine interpersonal discrimination, or the process of history against the hypostatisation of the moment, it consorts with radical political alternatives, appropriating for secular modern ends conventions much older in origin. Meanwhile, since *The Wild Goose Chase*, while offering itself as just such a quest-allegory with Marxist revolution as the goal in view, still continues on occasions to draw on that Romantic-symbolist legacy, to which the simplifying functions of allegorical techniques are anathema, the writing will be implicated in problematic countermovements to its main thrust.

A well-written allegory can offer the reader a chance to recover a number of pleasures and interests that are often lost or disdained in the rush for sophistication. There is a simple delight in following a story, in a writer's powers of sustained invention, in his or her creation of a complete and consistent world which the reader can inhabit with increasing confidence, however apparently bizarre its forms. Melville, a novelist who relished his allegorical flights, noted that 'it is with fiction as it is with religion; it should present another world, but one to which we feel the tie'.[2] In such a project

22

the fantasy is never a mere indulgence. 'Feel the tie' impressionisti-
cally marks a deep affinity between such inventions and reality,
enduring beneath what on the surface seems irregular or extravagant; an affinity of which the reader may become conscious, not
merely by way of some scattered recognisable landmarks, but
through a sense of the unfolding design and overall direction of
progress. One's interest can be both kindled and agreeably relaxed
by the initial address of allegorical narrative, promising as it
commonly does an expansive or enigmatic treatment of time, space
and physical laws. Within a world so open, local details can
provide the satisfactions both of surprise and of recognition, as if
by coming at something from an oblique angle one could both see
it afresh and know it instantly. The allegorist's technique of
continuous comparison itself arouses particular expectations, of a
message to be received or an inference to be drawn, giving
allegory an intellectual appeal beyond the imaginative quickening
which the convention of 'making strange' produces; the reader is
alerted to ways in which new light thrown on a notion or an event
may induce an altered judgement of it. And below this level of
relatively detached appreciation are rhythms in such narratives
which recall, even where they do not explicitly invoke, the experience of a certain kind of childhood; the pattern is at once unsettling
and consolatory, as successive disruptions and frightening encounters are felt to rest upon a base of deep security.

In this respect allegorical narratives can exhibit similar popular
formal properties as those which attracted Brecht, for example,
towards the idea of an epic theatre. They can present worlds in
which mysteries are there to be solved, with the reader or audience
invited to take an active part in their solution; the readership is
addressed as a mass; a significance is discovered for each moment
of experience; there are the beginnings of an alienation effect in the
alternation such narratives encourage between imaginative sympathy and judgmental distance. The characters of allegory tend to
find themselves in situations where complex moments of crisis must
be confronted and passed through; such occasions can be rendered
in bold outline and generalised, with an insistent push towards the
lives of the onlookers, implicitly questioning them, what would
you do? Which path would you choose? What factors are at work
in your choice? There can be a swift gathering up of dispersed and
accumulated elements into a momentary image of extraordinary
complexity and power, as, for example, when Gulliver listens

admiringly to the horses' parliament discussing his fate; there can be a sudden hardening of what was vaguely suspected into something concrete and unavoidable, as when Dante falls in a swoon at the story of Paolo and Francesca. Such occasions have more than merely didactic force; their simplicity is really a concentration of what has been recognised to be essential. Warner implies as much in his essay on 'The Allegorical Method', arguing that the two most effective uses of allegory were 'to give vigour and vividness to a definite belief', and 'to attempt fantastically to throw some light on what is beyond the ordinary reach of words'.[3]

A modern novelist, however, wishing to avail himself of allegorical conventions and their effects, has, as was mentioned, to work against the grain of outright hostility to allegory inherited from the Romantic period. Such hostility would issue in challenges from both the realist and the symbolist tradition. One committed to realism would argue that the relentless patterning of experience in allegory nails each event to its significance, abruptly cutting off its potential for growth or discussion. The fantastic landscapes in which items offer themselves for contemplation, their meanings not palpable in their form and texture but abstracted and intellectualised, while the real objects crumble in the hand – these may be seen as evasions of reality rather than as alternative expressions of it. The allegorist's style may seem to mix up, rather than to mingle, the naive and the rational, and become thereby too ponderous, too loaded with platitudes, an offence to sophistication rather than a calling of it to account. Most crucially perhaps for the liberal realist, the idea of the allegorical character, with its faith in the exemplary and the general, may seem to be merely a reduction of all subtleties and distinctions and a sacrifice of depth. Such an approach would appear culpably obsolete in the complex modern age, able to survive only in trifling or puerile genres such as romance or adventure-story, where certain facile conventions of characterisation remain to resemble decadent versions of the fixed compacts which supported allegorical writing in its feudal and Renaissance heyday (as, for example, the instantaneous recognition of another's rank in the chivalric code). The stress realism places on the uniqueness or impenetrability of the person appears incompatible with the idea of the allegorical type, or the representative figure, whose significance is ultimately available.

The sense that the meanings which arise from allegorical narratives have finite limitations is the essential ground also of the

Romantic-symbolist disdain for them. Gadamer summarised the view that came to prevail: 'Symbol and allegory are opposed as art is opposed to non-art, in that the former seems endlessly suggestive in the indefiniteness of its meanings, whereas the latter, as soon as its meaning is reached, has run its full course'.[4] Much of the early Romantic argument, that the route to the general lay through the vitality of the particular, expressed a strong (perhaps an implicitly democratic) reaction against an eighteenth-century vogue for personification and attitudinising; to a footnote in Reynolds's Discourses claiming on their author's behalf that a 'disposition to abstractions . . . is the great glory of the human mind', Blake rejoined 'To Generalize is to be an Idiot. To Particularize is the Alone Distinction of Merit'.[5] Allegory henceforward became increasingly associated with what was academic and mechanical; particularity and the autonomous character of the symbol, invested with the power to produce momentary revelation or access to eternal realities not otherwise to be grasped, now monopolised the forces of Imagination. The narrative forms of allegory, with their emphasis on patient movement towards specific objectives, are regarded by the Romantic mind as dull constrictions upon the freedom of the subject to explore its spontaneous identity with the world; not only are the meanings of allegory limited, but the act of interpreting them constrains the reader's individuality also. Hence at every turn in the development of nineteenth-century art the features of allegory are deemed to be beneath serious attention.

Some recent theoretical commentary on this development, most notably that of Paul de Man, has cast doubt upon the critical presumptions that underlay it. For de Man, the Romantic and post-Romantic privileging of the symbol was part of a deluded effort to bridge the gap between self and other, a yearning to enfold each within a single enclosure, which the methods of allegory, acknowledging as they do the difference between the sign and its referent, suggest to be unattainable. 'It remains necessary', de Man argued, 'if there is to be allegory, that the allegorical sign refer to another sign that preceded it . . . Whereas the symbol postulates the possibility of an identity or identification, allegory designates primarily a distance in relation to its own origin . . . in so doing, it prevents the self from an illusory identification with the non-self . . . the asserted superiority of the symbol over allegory, so frequent during the nineteenth century, is one of the forms taken by this tenacious self-mystification'.[6] The mystification is essentially the self's improperly considered anxiety to escape from the world of time. Walter Benjamin's conception of allegory also emphasised the 'decisive category of time',[7] which constituted its difference from the transcendent world of symbolism; in allegory, meaning is involved in history and reveals itself to patient contemplation rather than through spectacular intimations. Such abstruse revaluations of the tradition may seem portentous routes back to Rex Warner, but their appeals to the historical component of allegory, as a dismantling of inherited suppositions, does lend some general theoretical support to the alternative project for imaginative literature that Warner and his contemporaries were seeking, and to which he remained committed for 20 years.

For to those youthfully, uncertainly left-wing writers of the late 1920s, intent on a radical and often histrionic break with such modernist trends as they associated with the sterility and frustration of their world, allegory offered numerous advantages exactly where it was most inimical to both the liberal-realist and the symbolist traditions. To the radical view, the characters of bourgeois society are constructed out of the convergence of various forces. Hence allegory and typification, far from glossing over the distinguishing truths about such people, can penetrate what are held to be the merely superficial complications of individuality to discover their primary frame. The method could enable the radical writer to portray as typical and explicable precisely those aspects of personality which the liberal tradition would be most anxious to preserve as private and fathomless; the reader's attention would be directed away from the individual case towards the social function. In classic allegory of the kind Warner adopts in *The Wild Goose Chase*, the function of character is emphasised over its subjective life; the essential nature of the person is not distilled from self-communion, but exposed by the test of action and conflict. (The idea of subjecting oneself to a test, of distinguishing the 'truly weak' from the 'truly strong' man, had a special and well-documented appeal for many young intellectuals of the time, acutely conscious of having been born too late to fight in the First World War.[8]) The free movement of such allegory among ideas, and the illuminations that can derive from its incidental use of disjunction, exaggeration, the grotesque or the farcical, offer an alternative literary response to the world from that stressed in the predominant focus upon personal relationships and psychologies. There is in addition a vein of youthful censoriousness of their elders, common enough among the writers of Warner's generation, to which the allegorical method would also appeal; the sharp gestures of caricature preserve some of the impatience that provoked them. In the strongest examples from the tradition, such satirical portraits can become themselves suffused with some of the grandeur and scale of the allegorical project to which they are incidental; they can become not just mouthpieces for an idea, but independent embodiments of it, able to influence anew our sense of the experiences they touch on as much as can any avowedly 'realistic' character. The reality of figures such as Mr Worldly-Wiseman, or Uriah Heep, is displayed not in what might conventionally be called depth or subtlety, but in its opposite, in the immediacy and conviction with which they can be recognised as patterns to which the private experience of the reader is subsequently adjusted. And although none of Warner's characters has quite that durability and éclat, there are some – Don Antonio, Pushkov and Koresipoulos from *The Wild Goose Chase*, for instance – who come close to consummating the types they represent, and to making typology itself a newly relevant means of investigating human affairs.

Characterisation is only one of the features of allegory to offer possibilities to radical intentions. As Clifford and other commentators have pointed out, to adopt the forms of classic allegory is to commit oneself to certain presuppositions as to the nature of the world and the function and reception of literature within it.[9] Such a commitment would entail rather more than is typically included in the term 'parable-art', which Samuel Hynes used to characterise certain recurrent features of literature in the 1930s.[10] By classic allegory here is meant those narratives whose pattern is essentially the progress from doubt towards understanding, the quest to make the world intelligible. This was the form used most directly by Bunyan, variants of whose question 'What shall I do to be saved?' were the principal motivations of all Warner's allegories. Most modern allegorical writing is not of this kind. It derives more commonly from the dystopian tradition as problematically developed by Swift; or, it follows Kafka's influence towards fantasies of frustration and deflection from personal goals, to produce what Benjamin described as parables without a doctrine.[11] Warner incorporates into his work elements from both these familiar modern landscapes, and by the time of *The Aerodrome* (written 1939, published 1941) his use of allegory has come rather more to resemble theirs, but *The Wild Goose Chase*, on which he embarked well before the earliest translations of Kafka appeared in England, is still strongly attached to the older tradition. Its influence is manifested in various ways. The development of the narrative is progressive, and temporary hindrances and turnings-aside are understood to be so. The goal of rationality and intelligibility is always kept in view, and the range of meanings released by the signs encountered is not infinite. The hero's journey is firstly an education, by way of a number of exemplary trials and meetings, and subsequently a putting into practice of what he has learned. The story involves an ambitiously large scale of projection, because the gestures and declamations germane to the form need to carry across wide spaces, and not be confined, like intimate confidences, to an enclosed area. Most importantly, perhaps, for the radical writer, the meaning towards which the narrative proceeds should be both definite and collective; the pressures to fragment the response must be resisted, and the search should rather be to bind the readership into a clear community of understanding. The desire is for the leisurely unfolding of a pattern, sustained by the popular energies of satire and picaresque adventure, in which everything has a clear significance and nothing is beneath notice, and in which the values of the faith (here, socialist rationality), are consistently asserted in the face of experiences which threaten them. Warner suggested that allegory 'has been used with most remarkable effect by those writers who . . . have been most acutely conscious both of the grandeur and of the insecurity of their environment'[12]: those committed to a principle of order which might clarify and mitigate the insecurities while respecting the grandeur. The extent to which *The Wild Goose Chase* matches its expectations, or is waylaid by the traps it imagines itself to have adroitly skipped round, remains a question of considerable interest and suggestive implication.

The Wild Goose Chase was not published until 1937, but is nonetheless a very youthful piece; Warner had begun work on it as far back as 1929, possibly earlier, and the bulk was in manuscript by 1932. It presents a quest for the freedom and vitality which the bird of the title symbolises. The hero, George, is the youngest of three brothers who set out from their provincial town and cross a frontier into unknown lands to search for the Wild Goose. This semi-fabulous creature has been the object of much speculation and numerous earlier quests, though all seem to have foundered;

vague and variable meanings have been attached to it, all involving repressed desires and the sudden changes of fortune found in fairy tales. George travels last and slowest of the three. The characters he meets begin to define for him the political contours of the new country, and on one occasion, during a romantic interlude with Joan, the daughter of the leader of a peasants' revolutionary party, George hears the call of the geese in the distance. His pursuit takes him to the city which rules the land, a centre of tyranny and perversion which has established a stuffed goose as its idol; George's brothers, arriving there before him, have in different ways succumbed to the blandishments of the place, but he after desperate struggles manages to escape it. He returns to the country to rejoin the underground movement he had previously disdained, realising that the city and all it stands for bar the way to the open land beyond where the geese are calling him. Eventually the workers' army, with George at its head, defeats the city's forces; his two brothers, suitably chastened, return to the progressive camp, and the task of constructing a just society begins. George recognises, however, that many of the principal enemies have escaped, and the wild goose has not yet been securely discovered; the successful overthrow of tyranny was only a necessary stage in a quest not yet complete. The partial nature of his achievement was underlined early in the book by the return to the provincial town many years later of one purporting to be George, half-coherently exhorting the citizens to renew the quest themselves.

Such a bald résumé inevitably emphasises the naively comical elements in a book which is certainly not afraid to take risks. George encounters true and false routes towards the goal, and learns, in the course of what is presented as his personal and political maturing, to assess those things which impede or assist him. The idiomatic implications of the novel's title preserve the possibility that the quest may never finally succeed, and that all local achievements en route have to be measured against a persistent ideal demand; the story of George and his brothers is anticipated and to some extent determined by the pattern of previous quests, none of which takes possession of the promised land but rather bequeathes a fresh deposit of progress upon which subsequent aspirants are invited to build. Such complications remain in tension with George's apparently regular progress towards triumph; he travels across a spacious landscape where stylised conflicts are played out, between village and city, rebellion

and tyranny, human and mechanical power. The stylistic range
through which all this is delivered certainly indicates the length of
time occupied by the book's composition; passages of sustained
and serious argument intersperse with a certain amount of unfledged experimentation and less controlled satirical comedy. But
the kind of intelligence at work in the book is one characteristically
accompanied by a certain fatuousness – largely that of the young
idealist baffled by the apparent blindness of others to what he finds
self-evident; the novel is thereby kept going as much by the vigour
of its scorn as by the charm of its hope.

It begins with a traditional distancing device of allegory – an
introductory section which explains how the account of the hero's
adventures has been haphazardly reconstructed from fragments of
evidence by an attentive and self-effacing anonymous narrator.
The principal function of this convention is to give the narrative
that follows a doubtful, wondrous quality, holding it at a distance
that allows only certain kinds of question to be asked of it, and
leaves its meaning to be deciphered rather than discussed. In *The
Wild Goose Chase* the introductory material is split into two parts,
framing the quest between them; the first describes the departure
of the three brothers Rudolph, David and George, and the second
the return of the elderly man claiming to be George, from whom
the narrator haltingly collects his report. The narrator himself is a
representative of what Pound in 1933 called the mortmain, the
timorous and directionless post-First World War society, in need of
renewal but uncertain of both means and ends.[13] The description
of the brothers' departure is full of strain, provincial priggishness
mixed up with anxiety and disturbance; it betrays the narrator's
fascination with long trajectories of release, only barely suppressed
by his more complacent and official presentation of such feelings as
properly belonging to a youth at the memory of which wiser men
can smile. Eagerness for adventure is seen in the context of a
tradition of such enthusiasms, which has no need to examine
either its origins or its goal; the brothers' taking up the long-
standing quest for the Wild Goose is seen merely as conferring
lustre on the town they leave behind. Yet in the narrator's swirl of
participles is a yearning for a world of unbraced activity continuous
with his own, whose appeal is enticingly taboo:

Sailing on enormous wings that flashed in their high turnings
against the sun, long ribbons of light, or like the rims of metal

discs set firm and hardened in the velocity of steep falling, were
fishing the great pelagic gannets, seldom to be seen so clearly
with the naked eye. Over the cliff-face, facing eastward, helter-
skeltered strangely, like something supernatural, the ghostly
quick shadows of the screaming gulls; there seemed, though no
doubt it was only our excited nerves which made us think so,
an unusual restlessness of hurry in the natural scene and, for
relief and surety, we stared with new eyes at the sobriety of our
town architecture, the church's straight brown spire, the cobbles
in the square, and the sharp angles of the comforting exterior of
attics. (pp. 15–16)

The scene of the departure is subsequently acted out in a series of
allegorical tableaux whose implications escape the narrator.
Rudolph has an expensive motorbike but no petrol; George's pedal
cycle is old and rusty and about to be discarded; the town's police
force cannot chase him after his violent assault on the Prebendary –
a crude rejection of the codes of the hero's upbringing – because
none of their machines is roadworthy. Bergonzi, mistakenly sup-
posing that all three brothers were riding motorbikes, seemed to
assume that the book shared the town's admiration for the latest
transport technology, and that Warner was endorsing a kind of
futurist wanderlust with latent fascist implications. There is indeed
a disturbing right-wing undercurrent, as I shall suggest later, but at
this point it appears rather that the first stage of George's allegorical journey entails a rapid abandonment of such material
comforts, along with those who regard possessing them to be
sufficient guarantees of vitality. There is a similarly implicit challenge to bland comfort in respect of the narrator's assessment of
the characters of the three brothers. To him the intellectual David
seems a type of perfection; with a connoisseur's discrimination he
remarks that David's 'appearance was not so much effeminate as
indeterminate, expressing in one person the beauties of opposite
things, the male and the female, youth and age, sobriety and
licence' (pp. 20–1). But as the allegory develops it becomes clear
that this view will be regarded, not as a refinement of idealism, but
as a decadent blurring of lines that need to be clearly redrawn by
George's refusal to compromise. He does not negotiate pacts with
age, but angrily turns his back on it. At a later stage the feature of
the city which most appalls him is its enforcing of hermaphroditism among its élite – a condition to which David is already tending

and willingly accepts. These opening chapters are full of deliberately heavy ironies, enlisting the reader's support against the
presumptuous 'we' of the sterile settled community the narrator
represents. But the book does retain a hope that some of them at
least are still open to the appeal of the spirit of revolt, which is
momentarily stirred up by such occasions of public excitement.
The 'George' who returns, when asked if his quest was successful,
calls upon them to 'go into the marshes yourselves. Reclaim the
land. That's where you will find George' (p. 35). This closing of the
frame around the story maintains a classic allegorical structure, in
which the hero is ultimately absorbed or transfigured into an image
of the faith which is to be perpetuated by subsequent travellers.

Once George has passed beyond the influence of his home town,
and abandoned his bicycle, he begins a lengthy series of encounters with exemplary characters of the allegorical world. Amid the
various stylistic excursions in the writing one mode emerges which
will become increasingly dominant in Warner's later books, the
life-story or set speech of self-justification. But whereas in subsequent novels such occasions tend to be more tightly woven into a
dramatic framework, in *The Wild Goose Chase* whole episodes are
more casually inserted into the narrative, rather in the manner of
eighteenth-century digressions or nouvelles, in keeping with the
expansive and unhurried air of the book. The landscape through
which George travels mingles English with vaguely Middle Eastern
elements, doubtless deriving from Warner's first residence in
Egypt, between 1930 and 1932, when most of the novel was
written. In a later novel, *Men of Stones* (1949), a similarly exotic
setting will be used to challenge the insularity of the hero's
outlook; here, the composite geography produces rather a fantastic
exaggeration, sometimes for satirical effect but more strikingly to
gain the extra breadth this kind of allegory needs, the sense of
large tracts of open and uninhabited space between the scattered
personalities, which necessitates the simplified and declamatory
nature of their speeches about themselves, and gives the hero the
room he requires to move past and maintain his disengagement
from them. George meets three such characters in the no-man's-
land before crossing the frontier. Each of them represents for him a
different form of timidity or self-deception in the face of the
challenges that lie beyond. The opportunist musician Bob, a
refugee from the Jazz Age, has at least by virtue of his idiocy some
capacity for adaptation and survival, but the epicurean tyrant Don

Antonio, after proclaiming the delights of a pastiche Horatian retreat, commits suicide in belated recognition of its futility, and his brother Albert continues in the face of oppression to exercise a Christian patience, whose steadfastness George admires but which offers no hope of worldly redress. In the developing terms of the allegory, none of these three has had sufficient courage or independence of mind to cross the frontier, or to make commitments to life beyond the roles allotted them by what George regards as obsolete and sterile codes. His reaction to these characters and their stories is one of vigorous outrage and contempt, not yet organised into the consistent political diagnosis which the allegory will pursue.

Beyond the frontier, unknowingly crossed, George successively discovers the peasants' revolutionary party, riven by faction and dulled by its history of failure, and the insidious power of the city – a power expressed less through brutal coercion than through apparently random and cynical humiliations of the subject people. The end of George's education is the realisation that his individual prowess alone is incapable of reforming or even deflecting a force so ubiquitous and engrained. The bleakly comic oddities of the world are depicted with something of the youthful glee in caricature and technical juggling which animated much contemporary surrealism (one is reminded of the midget headmaster and the portraits coming to life in Vigo's *Zéro de Conduite*, as much as of the vaguely Kafkan elements which added colour to the later stages of the novel's revision). The surrealists may have regarded themselves as the vanguard of the Left, but despite the appeal of their methods to his fantasy and sense of fun, Warner does not wish to see surrealism as a radical challenge to natural perception. The political argument he relies on is rather as it came to be for Caudwell, that surrealist techniques were symptoms of the very decadence to which rational enquiry is opposed; in this specific instance, they are weapons used by the city to foist on its subjects a view of reality that accepts continuous distortion as the normal condition. Hence distances and durations vary according to the direction taken; characters are forced into isolation by the suspicions attending all relationships. It is hereabouts that the reader begins to sense that the political ambitions of the allegory are placed in implicit conflict with much of the episodic invention on which it is sustained; recurrently the writing in *The Wild Goose Chase* takes the form of a dogged war of attrition against the constant threat that consciousness will be overloaded by an excess of irrelevant or obscure material. Typically, a scene will take place, the contents peculiar to it will be displayed, and then its significance for the hero's progress will be recapitulated. Such a tactic involves much exasperating repetition, but its aim is to affirm a sanctuary, a moment of rest and reflection in which consciousness can step back from the arbitrary flow of events to consider and weigh up what of value can be gleaned from them. In a fairly characteristic example, after the revolutionary, Pushkov, has given a portentous and rambling account of his experiences in the city, those details which may have some future utility are sifted out and rehearsed:

> George had been attempting to adjust his mind to the complex-ities of Pushkov's story in such a way that he could receive some clear impression of the Convent in which, as he had been informed, his brother David was now residing, but the agitator had spoken so rapidly, had, by significant gestures, hinted at so much that he had not verbally expressed, that George was only slightly less ignorant than before, having learnt only that the Convent was a kind of Academy for young people, whose morals were, in Pushkov's view, unusually lax.   (p. 119)

Occasions such as these develop a standard device of allegory, whereby the questions asked of the natives by the traveller serve not only to release information but to distinguish the special objectivity the traveller possesses – however naive and raw it may be – from the natives' unconsidered or arrogant assumptions. In this case, the hero's maintaining a grasp on the essentials of any given encounter, in the midst of embellishments and red herrings, is a guarantee of his fitness for the quest. George's capacity for being educated into an understanding of Necessity is kept alive by his refusal to submit to the appeals of the immediate, which provide the force against which he must press to define himself. In contrast, and to underline the point, his brother Rudolph is shown to have surrendered to all the distortions and mystifications which the true questor's role is to dispel. George discovers a travel diary kept by Rudolph, in which a similar course of events as George has encountered – the meetings with the three characters before the frontier, with Joan, and the journey towards the city – is related in the manner of a Rider Haggard adventure; according to that convention the 'hero' imagines himself single-handedly to have overcome enormous odds and so proved his individual worth. But for the left-wing allegory, the true act of disenchantment, by which as if in a Jacobean masque the real hero puts to flight the falsehoods of magic and entrapment, comes about through the refining of scepticism into revolutionary purpose. Hence the affectionately parodic comedy of Rudolph's excursions is put into perspective by George's reaction to them; he insists on the typicality of Rudolph's narrative, the allegorical function of its delusions of grandeur, and thus undermines the idea of the isolated hero which it proposes, anticipating George's own later recognition that collective action alone can extract the individual from the dangers of solipsism.

Rudolph has been deceived by the extreme relativism which the city has inculcated in its subjects the better to control them. The abandonment of absolute standards has encouraged uncertainty and eventually heedlessness, not only of the concepts of time and space mentioned above, but of the value of all action. Such relativism, with its twin consequences of artificiality and sterility, increasingly emerges as the city's principle of organisation and source of power. Warner gives a vivid description of the place, drawing inspiration from Swift's Laputa and from the satires of Wyndham Lewis. The Convent and the Research Department are full of narcissistic aesthetes and obsessive scientists; the Anserium is a kind of Bauhaus cathedral for the officially-worshipped stuffed goose; there are lecture-halls with tiered seating sloping backwards, where hermaphrodite students laugh uncontrollably; the whole metropolis lives by floodlight under a concrete canopy. Warner's own background is perhaps betrayed by an excessive emphasis on educational and religious institutions, but some of the details of human experiments and artificial environments still strike a chord, however stale the scenery of megalomania has become since those days. But the State depicted here is in no strict sense fascist or Nazi; it is rather a life-denying oligarchy, full of inaccessible kings, disposable proletarians, disconcerting policemen and much apparatus for surveillance. Its attributes are not unified by a doctrine; it is the Enemy as it was at roughly the same time for Auden in *The Orators* – representing 'all those who distort and repress life, love and freedom', as Hynes briskly puts it.[14] (Those positive qualities to which it is opposed are marked allegorically by George's two encounters with the cry of the wild geese, on the occasions of his making intimate and unselfish contact with another person; once with Joan, once with the peasant-hero Andria.)

Warner finds some effective inventions to express the workings of this Enemy. A striking example is when Marqueta, the wife of a member of the Convent, seduces George in reverse, 'beginning with the consummation of passion and ending with a protest of fidelity to her husband' (pp. 196–7). This sharply mimes the Convent's ruling idea, that all actions and events have self-contained and repeatable outlines, which can be picked up and discarded at will, completely detachable from their meanings and consequences; no-one is thereby deemed responsible for anything. A slightly less exotic version of such a society is portrayed in *The Aerodrome*, except that there the hedonism runs alongside a strict military efficiency of a kind notably absent here. Within the terms of the allegory of Marxist education, the Convent represents the false freedom of absent restraint, whose attractions must be dismantled. Certainly such systematic perversions of humanity in the name of free experiment and the worship of the modern constitute a more formidable adversary than the provincial staleness George so promptly rejected – not least because, as with the surrealist comedy, the novel is clearly struggling with the fascination exerted on it by what it ostensibly opposes. Warner had launched into one fashionable experiment of his own, a grotesque stream-of-consciousness effusion at Joan's first entrance, which is unsure whether it is parodying its models (Joyce, Hopkins, Lawrence, and some inflections of rhythm and syntax from both Latin and Greek), or claiming their authority:

> Mouth broke to smile and eyes spilt sparkles . . . knowing the life coiled within . . . unreluctant to be cloistered, conscious of the oceanic soul tide-heaving through athletic limbs, of the million-volt spark to be generated later.   (p. 90)

– much the sort of thing admired by the despised literati at the Convent. But in the passages describing George's disconcerting experiences in the city, the insistence on a detailed exposition and recapitulation of every episode appears to derive exactly from the fear of surrender, not merely to an indiscriminate stream or flux of things, but to the kinds of fragmented, inconsequential, mechanical performances which in the world under attack are so readily substituted for natural ones. So what the novel eventually settles on as its characteristic style, a form of satirical and tough-minded bluffness reminiscent of Smollett, which can regularly appear so laboured and unsubtle, is really registering an anxious vigilance, an effort to safeguard the necessary amid the superfluous. It is determined to confront what is later called 'that difficult element, often of poison, which distinguishes what we think we know from what is' (p. 387), and to affirm that common agreements and rational understandings are still possible, for all the temptations to abandon them in favour of a life of private decadence divorced from growth or history.

The risk courted by such earnestness is of loss of momentum in the second half of the novel, where George begins to put into practice the radical insights he gained through his private tribulations earlier. 'Most allegorical heroes', Clifford writes, ' . . . are . . . most themselves when in pursuit of an object or struggling with their enemies'[15]; they need that continuous external pressure, the critical tension which holds character together. When George suspends his personal quest and devotes himself to the more anonymous and drawn-out task of organising a workers' uprising, the narrative loses the surge it needs to carry it over some of the problems caused by its ambitiousness. The section begins vividly enough with the story of Koresipoulos, a liberal sympathiser with apparently egalitarian aims, who betrays them at every point of difficulty. Warner's caricature here shows a crude, savage cutting-through of any impulse to tenderness or self-deception about such figures; a violent disgust against any sentimentalising about 'delicacy' and good will. But it emphasises how much more effective such allegorical characterisation is when applied to adversaries than when used to idealise the right-thinking. Andria, Joe and the other stout revolutionaries come ready-wrapped in moral clingfilm, disclosing a different kind of sentimentality on the part of their author – not coarse or wholly uncritical, rather a self-conscious diffidence arising from guilt at the legacy of middle-class condescension. The ambiguities of George's relationship with the workers' movement clearly reflect common anxieties of the early 1930s.

The question that pained was whether the truly progressive move was to join the workers by becoming one of them, giving up one's distinctive personality to merge with the crowd, or to join them by making common cause while retaining the critical detachment and 'individuality' inherited from one's liberal origins. The question still assumes that one's personal fulfillment is the principal goal; it derives again from Bunyan its concern not to waste or misdirect one's potential in times of crisis and uncertainty where it seems only one chance will be offered. The first alternative would claim that true self-fulfillment comes through dedication to the mass cause, as that alone can express what is fundamental and unifying in humanity, to which personal characteristics are mere luxurious accretions. The second is the more convenient alternative, as it preserves for the bourgeois intellectual a role in the progressive movement *qua* bourgeois, as a member of that élite breakaway group of the ruling class whose honourable mention in the Communist Manifesto was a favourite text of Warner's friend Day Lewis. The idea of the common cause maintained the flavour of romanticism, not far from Yeats's dream of a natural alliance between patricians and peasants against materialists and enemies of passion; there still seemed to be opportunities for heroism instead of mere sober calculations of advantage, and the detached élite held on to their qualities as leaders rather than humbling themselves completely.

George's uncertain status throughout these episodes marks the first stirring of Warner's interest in questions of leadership. In this case, George's detachment, and his lack of experience of the city's power and the opposition's failings, are regarded by the rank and file as strong qualifications for him to head their movement, since the other candidates are either exhausted by prolonged effort or tainted by their former connections with the enemy. This rather tends to suggest that the workers' army stands in need of the charisma, daring and sure instincts only provided by an independent officer class – another of those moments of romantic conservatism that underpinned the iconoclasm of the generation too young to have fought in the First World War. George's own appeal to his men runs contrary to this: 'It was an army of leaders, not of followers, who would take the town, and was not this the object of every leader worth the name, to render his own position of ascendancy unnecessary?' (pp. 285–6). His eye is fixed on the future establishment of an egalitarianism from which the State has withered away, when current disputes about who takes charge will be seen to belong only to a specific and past period of exigency. The future course actually depicted in the action of the novel, however, bears out the value of George's jealously-guarded independence from his working-class fellows (who mostly become victims of the kinds of bribery and corruption a number of the figures involved in the General Strike, or in Macdonald's government, were often snobbishly accused of having succumbed to), and projects less the triumphant levelling-up on which George rests his case for taking command, than the continuation of his incomplete personal quest for the wild goose, to which this revolution is only incidental. The unresolved conflict is between the values of adventure and those of settlement, whereby the individual has constantly to renew his challenge to any complacency on the part of the mass, and to fight the threat to his identity posed by any form of absorption.

Gobolov, the defeated leader of an earlier uprising, is clearest on this point: 'It is the love of life which makes the revolutionary . . . Keep yourselves whole. Never worship what you can touch. Help your comrades. Lead them, if you can, but do not love the mass, or you will betray it' (p. 298). He insists on maintaining freedom from all potentially corrupting attachments, on remaining disengaged and pragmatic about partnerships whose intensity might otherwise distract from the goal. These touches are clearly sub-Lawrencian, reminiscent in part of Birkin's constellated stars and of the antipathy to democratic sogginess in the essay on Whitman, and it appears to be the view *The Wild Goose Chase* wishes to endorse. Such revolution would have little to do with class solidarity, or economic analysis; its essential values would be religious or otherwise therapeutic, the recovery for the tradition of liberal humanism of the opportunity for purposeful action that had fallen from it in its decline. This view, as expressed by Warner and his fellows, was often and with routine disparagement called public-school Communism. Day Lewis, in *The Buried Day*, gave a becomingly modest retrospective account of his version of it[16]; it involved a good deal of precious agonising and mawkishness, but it was never mean-spirited or stupidly smart. There are passages of argument towards the end of *The Wild Goose Chase*, between George and David, or between George and Marqueta, in which the questions of liberalism's stagnation and its need to recognise the logical issue of its own projects are treated seriously; the opposing position is not cheapened or made to seem a mere rhetorical exercise to offset the hyperbole of the hero. Public-school Communism's emergence into literature had many puerilities, but was consistent enough to see that its moment of anxious transition from liberalism to socialism entailed genuine problems of creativity, to which allegory, in seeking collective significance for the personal quest, provided some progress towards an answer.[17]

The novel attempts to recover some of its earlier energy in the account of the revolutionary war, but here the writing becomes hamstrung by the demands of the allegorical scheme rather than invigorated by its possibilities. Warner does manage a certain amount of excitement, but, rather in the manner of Madame Mao's operas, plans are smoothly carried out or changed, commanders and soldiers alike have a clear view of the ground and its fortunes, and mistakes are caused by treachery and loss of nerve rather than by any circumstances more problematic and unaccountable. Such mythologising of battle conditions arose in part from the romantic notion many of Warner's generation had, that revolutionary war still offered chances for heroism and effective personal intervention almost completely lost to other forms of combat (a hope held by some who set out for Spain in 1936, but rapidly dispelled, well before the note of mild frustration at the ubiquitousness of danger and the absence of clearly demarcated lines which Isherwood, for example, sounded in his part of *Journey to a War*). Warner's battle is full of contrived emblematic encounters, between resourceful, lightly-armed men and inflexible mechanical monsters with Achilles' heels; the fighting is fanciful, and the scourging disgust of the earlier satirical sections sinks here to a more banal level of violent cruelty. Not only are the details expressed allegorically, but the whole course of the battle is predetermined by an allegorical interpretation of the historic destinies of those engaged in it. The defeat of the city is in this view inevitable, since in its complacency it had underestimated the forces ranged against it and had allowed its power to decline accordingly. The workers' victory is assured by the logic of the times, while marred somewhat by a number of prominent defections and the treacherous self-serving of some of George's less dedicated colleagues. The description of the course of events requires, however, a narrative interest to be worked into it rather at odds with the didactic intention; the battle is presented as to the very last a touch-and-go affair, as the writing tries to maintain suspense despite having deprived itself of any real uncertainties against which to define its progress. In allegorical passages of this kind, which are essentially demonstrations of something regarded as immutable, everything depends upon the prose's having sufficient colour to divert an attention which is otherwise wandering ahead; Warner's mostly does not. (Earlier in the novel, in one of the episodes of George's time in the city, there was a more interesting and strangely parodic version of this difficulty, in the account of the rugby match between the Pros and the Cons which George was made to referee. Here again the outcome of the fixture was known in advance, to all except George, but the players continued to perform as if it were not, in an obstinate defiance of the inevitable by which George was greatly impressed. The narrative here was half-comical, half-disturbing; the episode had a good deal of what Hynes referred to as 'schoolboy horseplay',[18] while clearly having been written by one who was himself a distinguished games player and not at all disposed to mock the values of the sports field. The passage was published by John Lehmann in *New Writing* in 1936, before the complete novel appeared.)

Such suggestions of a struggle against fate, in times not yet propitious, come to blend with the increasingly marked sense in the novel of George's destiny, of the tailoring of his apparently empirical and linear development to a predetermined, external pattern. During the uprising it is incidentally revealed that Don Antonio and Albert, whom George met and passed before crossing the frontier, and Joe, the elder statesman of the peasant's movement, comprised a former set of three brothers who undertook the quest for the wild goose, and who were either baulked by or fell into similar traps and temptations as have beset their successors. This feeding-back of what is cyclical or recurrent into a narrative of ostensibly clear progress has something of a double effect. It allows on the one hand for the application to present times of what has been learned from previous unsuccessful efforts, when the long winter of the revolution awaited its spring. On the other hand it limits the hero's freedom of manoeuvre and the integrity of his personal discoveries; he is constrained not only by current conditions but by the role marked out for him – registered in the novel by the mysterious imprint of a webbed goose-foot on his mother's skin. (In a disguised and undeveloped fashion, his quest contains an element of the search for the lost father that becomes a more powerful compulsion in *The Aerodrome*.) George is not only the successful revolutionary leader, whose political consciousness was raised by the grafting onto his good intentions of a sound and rational grasp of Necessity. He is also the third brother of the fairy tale, the one who, classically, overturns conventional expectations to accomplish what, unbeknown to him, he was appointed to do.

Hence an undercurrent of conflict is maintained, just as had been felt in the forms taken by the writing, or in the ambiguous relationship between the individual and the mass: the urge towards adventure and expansion, towards a spontaneous breaking of constraints, runs alongside the need for order and clarity, a framework to which each moment in the allegorical progress must be fitted for its real significance to be secured.

This tension is established and to an extent controlled by the alternative endings of the novel: the spectacular triumph over the city, and the subsequent half-madness and disappointment of the 'George' who returns. Controlled, because such a structure could accord with Marxist projections of the stages through which continuous revolution must pass; the eventual coldness and brittleness of the hero's position, after struggling so long to maintain detachment from the psychological impact of what he had to confront, would be part of the price to be paid for the future prospects of others. In these terms the allegory of progress towards faith retains its vigorous forward thrust, which the conflict between adventure and settlement helps to generate. But there remain more problematic ways in which the tension is registered. In the climactic moment, where the victory is asserted of the forces of reason and clarity over obfuscation and the stasis of luxurious bemusement, something leaks back into the language that had sought to seal itself:

> Now, looking upwards, they saw the whole blue sky and the sun, and across the sky streaming the white shapes of flying birds, a horde, from horizon to horizon; nor was their number more to be wondered at than the size and splendour of each one of them; for these creatures were altogether uncommon, with wings wider than playing-fields, bodies like boats, and straight extended necks like a flying forest. From close down and brilliant pinions the light shone in a dazzling whiteness or was refracted in every rainbow colour, with a glint of gold behind the stern black of each powerful advancing bill. Very slowly and in complete silence the birds passed, going like galleons, huge ships with sails set and filled majestically by some wind that blows beautifully on the sea, though the watcher on the shore stands in admiration with not the smallest breeze to fan his cheek. And so for mile after mile and for a time that no one could reckon the enormous wild shapes of beauty and of strength went

over the army, and George looked reverently at the white flying
and at the men beneath it.   (p. 441)

The voice here is that of the mannered, excited narrator of the
novel's opening; the mode employed is symbolist fantasy, repro-
jecting into the writing much of the indefiniteness of meaning and
excess of activity which George's progress had sought to control.
The most important political task had been the attack on
hermaphroditism, the clear redrawing of lines which had been
blurred. But here, while the geese appear to fly over in a kind of air
force salute, their origin and destination remain unclear and the
narrator's perception of them uncontrolled; the rhetorical piling-up
of awe rather takes the place of than complements the jubilation
underneath. Hence at the moment of revolutionary triumph there
is a partial return to the beginning, in the narrative's anxiety to
assert its will over phenomena whose meanings remain beyond its
scope. The language is not able to express the altered way of seeing
the world which the revolutionary argument demanded. It can
only call for renewed effort, and hope that its vigour and sweep
can hold off the persistent doubts – as to whether the quest could
ever be fulfilled, whether the freedom George seeks is real or
illusory, whether the spirit of adventure that is needed to initiate
the quest could ever find a secure home among those on whose
behalf the quest is undertaken; whether, indeed, as the closing
pages themselves rather question, the capitalist world is really so
far in decline that a moderate blow will flatten it.

There are other, related tensions in addition to the inconsistencies of argument and method. At some moments of allegorical
invention there is a relish which, though not damagingly affecting
the judgement, betrays a vein of sympathy for things which the
moral vision of the book cannot allow itself to accept. It is more
than a matter of evil's being more interesting than good, or the
need in allegory to show the enemy as endlessly and insidiously
proliferating. There is an evasiveness about some of the reactions
that is not bought off by the bluffness with which they are
dismissed. When we read Rudolph's diary, Koresipoulos reciting
his Ode to Speed, or the rugby team's lament for its murdered
captain, we sense that parody is holding at arm's length certain
feelings which are closely connected to those the novel wishes to
promote, but for which no language other than parody is readily
available. Similarly convenient is George's rejection of Marqueta at

the end of the story. What begins as a conflict between feeling and moral approval is simplified by Joan's timely return; her less demanding sexuality dispels Marqueta's seductive visual appeal and makes George's decision too easy. What is at stake there is George's unacknowledged cult of the masculine, flinching defensively from anything clinging or emotionally complex; it has its own timorousness, disguised as the leader's obligation to remain disengaged from personal burdens.

The book does convincingly discuss some aspects of this proximity of rival or contrary responses, in the account of David's life at the Convent, where the absence of any checks on his freedom led him towards insanity; hereabouts Warner shows what he has learnt from Dostoyevsky (the resemblances between David and Ivan Karamazov are stronger than those of the other sets of brothers). But the contraries emerge more interestingly when they are less obviously under the author's control. When George gives a lecture at the Convent on *Othello*, he argues that 'the most pronounced of Shakespeare's moral feelings' are

> an undeviating contempt for people who are merely clever, for partial reports, for low aims, for split minds, and correspondingly an unlimited admiration for those who, however mistakenly, follow a grand idea and are fanatical, ingenuous, pig-headed.
> (p. 186)

The flourish of adjectives at the end – George is trying to shock his students into listening – serves perhaps to distance him slightly from a full confrontation with his meaning: that there exist great men whose vitality and colour derives from an inflexible will. Although the allegory insists that the plight of an Othello belongs to a phase of history which has now been surpassed, that though 'a figure of great and noble simplicity' he was 'terribly ruined by contact with a completely false system of values' (p. 185), nevertheless the allure remains of the 'grand idea' as something necessarily running against the grain of such common agreements and beliefs as the socialism in the novel founds itself on. The object of the Leader, as George claimed, may be to render his ascendancy unnecessary, but the novel can never quite reach the point where individual distinction is voluntarily relinquished.

Such a concern with the will and its powers can enter the very texture of the writing. It was suggested earlier that one of the satisfactions offered by allegory lies in the balance it can maintain between imaginative involvement and intellectual scepticism. When judgement of a situation or issue is called for, it is thereby passed on the evidence of a full hearing. But while it seeks to exert a provisional control over these two distinct responses, much allegorical expression may itself be issuing from a more complex, less well-marshalled fusion of identity and detachment. De Man's argument was essentially that identity – symbolism – was deconstructed by detachment – allegory, but none of the terms of such relationships can be fully disposed of. The yearnings for absorption which Romantic symbolism manifested return to haunt the efforts to suppress them. On the one hand, the allegory Warner uses is a means of rescuing consciousness from the threat of submersion. It can provide a breathing-space, a vantage point from which the reason can recover from its buffetings and exercise itself against the flux. Allegory does this by locating the meaning of experience not in the moment of its occurrence, but in its relationship to the larger canvas on which it settles, or the grid through which it is measured. Hence the needful is sifted from the superfluous, and meaning becomes finite and practical, related always to the clear objective. But on the other hand, such allegory may equally be expressing an anxious desire that there should be such order and pattern; that in the absence of a secure covenant the will must strive to create a meaning, through chosen and significant interlockings, as much as to discover and reveal one. Standing aloof from the object and imposing oneself on it in a possessive seizure may be as it were two sides of the same coin, denoting the mind's implicit defence against the onset of sheer quantity. Georg Simmel in one of his essays suggested that the tragedy of modern man was that he was surrounded by too many cultural signs to be assimilated, but that he could never give up trying to assimilate them, since they were all potentially implicated in his development;[19] clearly it is no accident that modern allegory should readily consort with the depiction of alternative or science-fiction societies which have worked to reduce that number of signs, and reduce the differences between their members, so that the one may more easily stand for the many. The impulse towards allegory, however powerfully satirical its account and however vehement its rejection of such worlds – as Warner's undoubtedly is – is unlikely to escape altogether a certain complicity with them in the deep levels of its organisation. In *The Wild Goose Chase* Marxism goes some way towards providing a unified global view, an optimism that one could be achievable, of which allegory can remain an enthusiastic servant. But Warner's Marxism was a heady brew, and had a number of potentially fascist elements mixed in it; not the ones Bergonzi mentioned, but some incidental values emerging from the book – cleanliness, athletic grace, rural purity, unsophisticated sex – which were either uncomfortably close to fascism or subsequently found themselves so firmly taken over by it as to be virtually irrecoverable for anything else. The sincerity of the book's intentions, and the appropriate fitting, for the most part, of the method to the matter, carry the reader past much of the doubt; but the cumulative effect of the various tensions reveals a latent instability between the democratic and the totalitarian implications of the allegorical method, an instability which becomes more influential as Warner's career develops. And even in this novel, where his socialism is most ostensibly committed, it is easy to sense that one of the reasons his works project so powerfully the imaginative appeal of fascism is that he was himself strongly attracted to it.

Notes

1. Bernard Bergonzi, *Reading the Thirties*, London 1978, p. 84.
2. Herman Melville, *The Confidence-Man*, standard edition, New York 1963, p. 244.
3. Rex Warner, 'The Allegorical Method', from *The Cult of Power* (1946), p. 110.
4. Hans-Georg Gadamer, *Truth and Method*, trans. Barden and Cumming, New York 1975, p. 67; quoted in Paul de Man, 'The Rhetoric of Temporality', from *Blindness and Insight*, London 1983, pp. 188–9.
5. William Blake, *Annotations to Sir Joshua Reynolds's Discourses*, in *William Blake's Writings*, ed. Bentley, volume 2, Oxford 1978, p. 1458. Marina Warner notes additionally the eighteenth-century enthusiasm for Hesiod's *Theogony* as a rediscovered source of allegorical types, in her *Monuments and Maidens*, Pan Books, London 1987, p. 70.
6. Paul de Man, *Blindness and Insight*, pp. 207–8.
7. Walter Benjamin, *The Origin of German Tragic Drama*, trans. Osborne, London 1977, p. 166. There is an enlightening discussion of these notions in Julian Roberts, *Walter Benjamin*, London 1982, especially pp. 140–148.
8. The point, particularly as described by Isherwood, is concisely related by Samuel Hynes in *The Auden Generation*, London 1976, pp. 126–7.

9. Gay Clifford, *The Transformations of Allegory*, London 1974, p. 36.
10. Hynes, *The Auden Generation*, pp. 13–15.
11. Walter Benjamin, *Illuminations*, ed. Arendt, trans. Zohn, London 1970, p. 122.
12. Rex Warner, 'The Allegorical Method', pp. 119–20.
13. Ezra Pound, 'An ABC of Economics', in *Selected Prose 1909–65*, ed. Cookson, London 1973, p. 226.
14. Hynes, p. 182.
15. Clifford, p. 21.
16. C. Day Lewis, *The Buried Day*, London 1960, pp. 209–11.
17. There are interesting comments on the idea of a rational rather than sentimental commitment to left-wing literary practises in an essay by Arnold Rattenbury, 'Total Attainder and the Helots', in *The 1930s: A Challenge to Orthodoxy*, ed. Lucas, Harvester Press 1978, pp. 138–60.
18. Hynes, p. 36.
19. Georg Simmel, 'On the Concept and Tragedy of Culture', in *The Conflict in Modern Culture and Other Essays*, trans. Etzkorn, Teachers College Press, Columbia University, New York 1968, p. 44.

3

The Professor

When at the age of 17 I read *The Professor* for the first time I was impressed most forcibly by its seriousness. Here was a work of fiction dealing strong-mindedly and with no superfluous embellishment with matters of the first importance. This quality of seriousness did not derive simply from the contents or the occasion of the novel – the takeover by fascist forces of a minor European democracy. It was rather that the novel seemed to take its form directly from the circumstances it was engaged with, so that their terrible immediacy and closeness was respected even in the act of providing a perspective from which they might be more clearly viewed. The rapid succession of vehement arguments, the sudden gleams of clarity extinguished by chaos and betrayal, enabled the novel to convey by means of its tone and structure, over and above its particular details, the atmosphere of a small, landlocked country, enclosed on all sides by hostile forces, breaking out in civil war, and offering no hiding-place from the overwhelming pressures. Amid all this the main character tries to cling, with increasing desperation, to his beliefs and his identity, as if to a raft in a whirlpool. This imaginative grasp of the mood of the situation, as much as the efforts to discriminate the issues and forces at work in it, seemed to me to constitute what I thought of as the book's 'European' dimension. It was not cosmopolitan and wide awake by virtue of its subject alone; nor, I think, was I simply exercising upon it a priggish sixth-former's discovery of 'European' sophistication, of a literature of darker recesses and more fascinating obsessions than were usually found at home. It was that despite recognisably English elements, of landscape description and satirical comedy, the novel had thrown off that protective insularity, that retention of a secure parochial patch from which one could observe such events and on which, however hypnotic and appalling their appearance, their full force would never be unleashed. What happened in the novel was not to be experienced as a spectacle alone, but as a mêlée in which one was exposed on all sides. *The Professor* would one by one touch on areas traditionally associated with relaxation from major stresses – pastoral retreat, untainted personal relationships, endearing eccentricities of manner – only to reveal them as constructed by and implicated in the very forces they sought to evade. The restraint and clarity of much of the prose reinforced this sense of an austere confronting of what was painful and inevitable, making the reader more acutely aware of how precious was his own space for reflection.

This severity, lack of false sentiment, and evenness of the prose mark considerable changes from *The Wild Goose Chase*, and answer to a number of the points Samuel Hynes makes about the general character of later-1930s political literature. He argues that the tone of apocalyptic struggle is maintained and even heightened, but that its focus shifts from that of the impending communist overthrow of capitalism to that of a communist-led Popular Front against fascist tyranny. Thereby a good deal of the exuberant attack dwindled away from political writing, to be replaced by an essentially defensive strategy; the struggle was now seen rather as the sole means of preserving what was worthwhile in human existence than as a progress towards a radically new form of life. Such a transition would not have been wholly uncongenial to those, like Warner, whose socialism was always strongly related to its liberal ancestry, but the need to clarify that relation, and to recognise the significant differences, was now more urgent than before. *The Professor* just holds on to the tone of early-1938, the faintly surviving hope that some effective action can still be taken to halt the advance of barbarism and prevent a world war, but the hope is presented grimly and with great wariness.

Another point made by Hynes is that as the detail and scale of the atrocities actually being committed became more widely known, much of the fantasy and exaggeration that had characterised political writing earlier in the decade gave way to a more sober realism. There was a moral concern to bear witness to the truth, rather than a beggaring of the imagination by reality; the imagination was used to shape the gathered material, which arrived ready-disturbed and no longer required disturbance to be worked into it. Hynes, developing his idea of 'parable-art', picks up a distinction Spender drew between 'reportage' and 'fable', to suggest that 'in the best writings of the thirties, the two ... interweave',[1] and this is true of *The Professor*, if we allow 'reportage' to include the kind of fictional representation of contemporary events on which Warner's narrative is grounded. Incidental details which *The Professor* reproduces in its own form, such as the way Austrian Jews were forced to use their own clothing to scrub the streets clean of pro-independence slogans, were well known and widely reported at the time. For Warner, however, the element of 'fable' must retain the upper hand in any such interweaving: 'It is becoming clear that if pure fantasy, unrelated to reality, is dangerous, lunatic and irresponsible, pure observation, undirected by imagination or moral impulse, is almost meaningless'.[2] The organising techniques sought by his allegorical method, of placing, foreshortening, and concentrating of essentials, are for him necessary to reveal the true significance of the bare details and prevent the reaction to them from being merely inert or vicarious. Meanwhile the reader is brought to confront the issues and ideas that arise from such material through the developing predicament of the hero, whose place in the surge of events forces him to face directly things which would otherwise have remained subjects for detached and distant speculation. In comparison with *The Wild Goose Chase* or *The Aerodrome*, *The Professor* is rather a 'novel of ideas' than a fully furnished allegory; it retains the typical method, of the exemplary narrative set in an imaginary country, but the political and moral arguments take precedence over any continuous symbolic invention.

Part of the youthful optimism of *The Wild Goose Chase* was conveyed by the constant prospect of breaking out, from moments and scenes of constriction into a huge, uncluttered landscape of possibility, of high skies and long horizons. By contrast, *The Professor* presents a closing-in of things; of characters being pressed into ever-tighter confinement, of spaces being invaded and occupied, of minds becoming overstrained and unstable. This contraction of possibilities affects the text in various ways. However deeply divided by their ideological convictions, the characters in *The Professor* all recognise that crisis is at hand, that history has caught up with them. They may propose radically different responses to it, but the fact itself binds them into a proximity quite different from the widely-dispersed positions articulated in *The Wild Goose Chase*, and underpins the more consistent tone of the writing here. The lack of room for manoeuvre compared with the earlier novel, the loss of the epic distances that enabled the characters to disengage from each other and move on, brings with it also a new element of compassion and a fundamental, if frail, solidarity. The shared experience of disaster creates a different kinship from one exclusive to a class or asserted from logical deductions. It is notable that while *The Wild Goose Chase* began with the wholesale and violent rejection by the young man of the society of his upbringing, the action of *The Professor* starts with a firm but respectful challenge of the father by the son; the conflict of argument is informed by strong family feeling as well as a more objective mutual esteem. In various ways the book brings into play certain connections between the protagonists which lie beyond their accidental colliding with each other, forces of attraction beyond historical necessity alone; they are never fully lit, but remain dim suppositions within scenes too rapid to permit further exploration.

This new bareness and cramping of the fictional project is not without risks. Occasional moments of melodramatic contrivance, where an allegorical diagram rather intrudes upon a scene than emerges convincingly from it, can seem more awkward here than in the course of a quest that can touch lightly on such things and leave them. When young Jinkerman rescues the Professor from a Nazi assailant, the spreading of the bloodstain onto the leg of the Professor's writing table is, as Arnold Rattenbury pointed out,[3] a nice symbolic touch; but the miniature allegory of the whole scene, in which the quick and decisive action of the communist rescues the liberal simultaneously from a fascist threat and from an impasse created by his own impotence, does seem, in the context of the seriousness of the arguments which led up to it, rather thin and heavy-handed. Katharine Hoskins (whose critique of this novel's political analysis is founded upon a peculiarly American faith in the resilience of democracy) suggests that in *The Professor*'s more 'realistic' narrative the caricatures are harder to accept than in the more extravagantly fantastic world of *The Wild Goose Chase*.[4] I think this is true of some minor figures, like the trade union leader and the pacifist priest, who are not given speeches of sufficient distinction to mitigate the effect of their transparency as characters. But the novel is committed to an urgent consideration of the most pressing claims, leaving time for only the briefest attention to others. It is not simply that a 'novel of ideas' is more concerned with arguments than with the detailed portrayal of those who argue. It is that the form and manner of the narrative aim to be commensurate with the necessities of the material; the urgency of current political demands takes precedence over such fine discriminations among individuals as proceed from the very position of liberal privilege that the times have rendered untenable. The struggles of the central character to hold on to this position are, it is argued, not merely impractical, but a culpable misuse of his advantages, contributing to the destruction of all that he holds dear. The novel wants to insist that conditions for the free and useful expression of what remains valuable in the liberal character can only be restored by a socialist revolution, during which the particular concerns of the individual must of necessity be set aside. It follows for Warner that a 'novel of ideas', in which certain personal distinctions are sacrificed for the sake of a clearer presentation of the general issues, is in this case the most appropriate form of literature available.

The novel presents forceful and lucid arguments, and much of the narrative has an immediate impact. But it is implicated in something deeper and more problematic than its own propaganda. Hynes noted the sense of tragedy, despite the narrative's best efforts, in the character and career of the defeated hero[5]; the whole relationship between the novel's point of address, to an as yet unrealised post-revolutionary and post-tragic society, and the play of values and aspirations within the events recounted, supplies the work with levels of interest beyond those of its immediate priorities. The stance the novel deliberately takes is shaded rather than impugned by such enduring complications.

The stance is made clear in the introductory passages of the novel, and the shading accompanies it from the beginning. Warner repeats the allegorical convention of *The Wild Goose Chase*, whereby the story is pieced together from surviving evidence by an anonymous narrator. But whereas in the earlier novel the narrator remained uncertain of the meaning of the events he described, and stayed outside the circle of the enlightened, in this more straitened world things are quite different. This narrator seeks to establish from the outset a dominant judgmental tone, which implies no doubt that the significance of the story has been fully digested, and that its unfolding will be an exemplary demonstration of the errors which the wiser society of readers will avoid:

> Those who knew the man seem to have admired him, though pity rather than admiration is likely to be the feeling by which those who peruse his history will be most affected; for we shall see a man quite unfitted for power, in his day the greatest living authority on Sophocles, rich in the culture of many languages

and times, but for his own time, not through irresolution or
timidity but rather, as it seems to us, through a pure kind of
blindness, most inapt. He believed against all the evidence,
scholar though he was, not only in the existence but in the
efficacy of a power more human, liberal, and kindly than an
organisation of metal. He believed not only in the utility but in
the over-riding or pervasive power of the disinterested reason.
Metal was to be proved harder than his flesh, stupidity and
fanaticism more influential than his gentlest syllogisms; and yet,
easy though it is to name the man a pedant and dismiss him as
misguided, his contribution to a civilisation that may one day be
organised or given room to flower will be found, perhaps, to
have been not altogether *nil*.   (pp. 13–14)

This is the voice of the continuing struggle, of the newly-
emerging State, anxious to promote pragmatic rather than idealistic responses in its model citizens. The narrator introduces the
Professor as a man capable of arousing a certain respect even
among his detractors. But it is 'pity rather than admiration' that is
felt by 'us', towards those guilty, according to these new standards, of 'a pure kind of blindness', and of bestowing upon
'disinterested reason' a status higher than mere 'utility'. The
writing tacitly acknowledges the danger that a heroic failure might
be admired as well as pitied, on the grounds that the old societies
he represented were vitalised as much as corrupted by the conflicts
which the new rational state would resolve. Hence room is left for
further development, a future when the pressures will relax and
allow the new culture to assimilate the best aspects of those who
are presently behindhand in their thinking. The passage also
sounds the first note of complication in the novel's view of the
liberalism the Professor embodies. 'He believed against all the
evidence, scholar though he was', suggests that the Professor was
not, after all, a sufficiently rigorous scholar; it appears that some
inner weakness or flaw prevented him from putting into practice
the tenets of objectivity and rational judgement which he upheld,
and that had he done so, he too would have accepted the narrator's
conclusions. Socialism thus hints at being liberalism in action,
bringing with it the appeal of a revived classicism which would
once again close the gap between the intellectual and the practical
life. The play of alternative attitudes towards the traditional
classics becomes a recurrent feature of the text.

It is consistent, moreover, with the relentless exposure else-where in the novel of hitherto safe places, that the critique of liberalism should in part be conducted in the very heart of liberal territory, the humanism derived from Greece. Already as the narrative begins the independent security the Professor enjoyed in his academic life has been invaded. Rumours of his impending appointment as head of the Government lead the students attend-ing his lecture to judge 'not so much the poems of Sophocles as the critic of the poems, and judging him not as a critic, but as a man' (p. 15). It is known that such power as the Professor could wield would not rest on any large-scale party or class support, but on his personal integrity and his favourable reputation abroad. Any success he might have would arise rather from his appearing as a rallying-point for those of good will, than from his actuating new or radical initiatives. Hence much is evoked by the text of his lecture, the lines from *Oedipus Tyrannos* in which the Priest be-seeches Oedipus to take it upon himself to save the city from its pollution. The Professor's response to his own allusion is charac-teristic, as later instances will confirm. Without pausing to consider any ominous analogy between his own situation and the context of these lines, he proceeds to expatiate upon the democratic organisa-tion of the Polis, by way of a second, comparable passage – 'very similar words spoken in a quite different situation' (p. 19), as he himself remarks. His classicism tends to be generalised and idealistic; it draws more deeply on the emotional appeal of glittering scenes and stirring declarations than the rationalism he educes from it is keen to acknowledge. It may be that his impres-sionistic method is employed here to appease his students' love of slogans, but it does not prevent an outburst by his own son, who immediately places the real developments of history in direct opposition to his father's faith in universals. The son argues that this abstract notion of the Polis is irrelevant on two counts: it has no practical relationship with present conditions, and such demo-cracies as do exist have been corrupted and betrayed by their own leaders. Consequently the main issue of the book is joined; 'there is no enclosed space in Europe' (p. 22). (We might catch, in the son's claim that the Professor and his kind bear responsibility for the present distresses, a faint echo of Teiresias's revelation to Oedipus, that the one who seeks to solve the problem is actually the cause of it – a view expressed later from different positions by the fascist Vander and the ascetic Christian Jinkerman senior.)

The argument heats up when a student Nazi intervenes, but here in the lecture-room the Professor can still exercise power; he can present an even-handed summary of the propositions and maintain the forms of rational debate, even when he feels that the debate itself has been animated by unconsidered sentiment. But as will shortly be made even more obvious, the enclosed space of the Polis is now bounded by the university walls. In his closing remarks, the Professor once more appeals to his students not to allow their rational judgements to be clouded by feeling; this time his text is the first stasimon of the *Oedipus*, where the chorus fights down its inclination to assert Oedipus's guilt on the strength of Teiresias's accusation alone. 'Never by the verdict of my heart shall he be adjudged guilty of crime', as Jebb translates it. The Professor evidently regards this as a noble upholding of principle in the face of panic and emotion; others might equally see it as an instance of blind faith, an adherence to an inappropriate idealism which impedes the grasp on reality. The chorus had earlier lamented its inability to discover a practical remedy, and had resorted instead to desperate prayer, as 'thought can find no weapon for defence' (Jebb); Warner's narrator implies in his turn that the Professor's position is not so much clear-headed and wise as inadequately engaged and thus helpless:

> The smile on his lips as he looked at the angry excited faces showed his wish to understand and to help rather than any real understanding or ability to resolve emotional conflicts which, though he admitted them to be genuine, could not but seem to him somewhat indecent. (p. 24)

There is a division in him between the intellect and the blood, which does not work wholly to his advantage. The effort he makes to subdue what he sees as his grosser nature in the interests of a higher claim is part, too, of what divides him from his own classical models. By habitually abstracting his favourite passages into general pronouncements, he not only ignores some implications of the contexts from which they are torn, but also undervalues (as he himself will later admit) the degree of integration between those ideals and the society that produced them – that element which cannot so readily be transferred from their time to his. There are more ways than one of interpreting Greek ideas, and the Professor's has his own virtues, of consistency and courage. But the

narrator closes this first chapter by projecting a different tone, of
one who truly understands what is real, and the compromises of
integrity needed to deal with it. The appeal to objective judgement
here is conducted by way of some Brecht-like distancing and
erasure of suspense:

> He did not know that beyond the frontier the enemy's plans had
> been completed three weeks ago. He did not suspect the
> treachery of the Chief of Police ... It could hardly be supposed
> that a man of his character would have acted differently, nor is it
> likely that, however he might have acted, events would have
> been in any material sense altered. What is perhaps remarkable
> about the Professor is that, even supposing him to have possessed
> at this time the fullest information, he would not, in all proba-
> bility, have departed in any important respect from the course
> which he actually pursued.   (p. 31)

The narrator has by now outlined the general situation, argued
proleptically the unlikelihood of any individual's having a significant impact on it, and introduced the Professor as one whose
concerns are so distant as to make his chances even weaker than
most. At the same time, the tone of slight wonder in the above
passage – 'perhaps remarkable', 'in all probability' – recalls that of
the earlier assessment: 'He believed against all the evidence,
scholar though he was, not only in the existence but in the
efficacy of a power more human, liberal, and kindly than an
organisation of metal' (p. 13). This tone seems simultaneously to
invite an ironic reading and to ward it off; on the one hand the
narrator's own 'organisation of metal' is momentarily challenged
by that depth of trust, and on the other the direction of desire
seems to vacillate between radical pragmatism and a nostalgia for
older, simpler worlds. The interplay throughout of allusion and
commentary begins to establish the Professor as a tragic figure,
whose flaws remain a measure of his humanity, even as the
narrator enjoins us to see them as restrictions upon it.

In the second chapter, the Professor passes through his college
gates into a less exalted world. In presenting it the narrative
employs a similar kind of Fieldingesque bluffness to that developed in *The Wild Goose Chase*, in keeping with its desire to tell the
time rather than to examine the mechanism of the watch. Hence
the ironic juxtapositions and threatening contrasts are so vigorously

underscored that they could not possibly be missed. This imaginary country's equivalent of Speakers' Corner, the second 'enclosed space' for free speech, is occupied by cranks while bombers manoeuvre overhead. While the Professor is exasperated by the fatuousness of what is being said, he seems not to notice how marginal and irrelevant such freedoms seem to be in the world outside his own. The mood of vague, Micawberish uncon- cern with which the country carries on its life on the brink of crisis emerges as convincingly from the satirical picture as does the Professor's mild bewilderment at it; Warner's method is to select a small detail to stand for and illuminate the whole. A gas-mask salesman is blithely promoting his stock; the Professor is forced momentarily to wonder how far the conditions of earning a living set constraints on behaviour and opinions: 'Was it that the nature of his job ... demanded ... an expression of semi-idiocy, an overweening confidence that no sane person could possibly feel?' (p. 37). But the Professor still believes that the crowds applauding him outside the Chancellory are genuine, and that the man who attempts to assassinate him is, however curiously, at least inde- pendently motivated. Even the revelation by his assailant, the communist Sergeant Jinkerman, that the whole affair was staged for propaganda purposes by the Chief of Police, fails to shake the Professor's faith that the self-evident justice of his cause will itself provide him with the liberty of action to which he is accustomed.

Jinkerman regards this faith as a fantasy no less ludicrous than those of the park speakers. Those figures, like the ministers the Professor subsequently meets, are flatter and less vibrant carica- tures than their counterparts in *The Wild Goose Chase*. The broad slapstick effects of left-wing writing, attempting to draw on popular theatrical traditions and their associated prejudices, re- quire for their success a context of more leisure than this novel is able to give them. Here instead a certain brusque impatience with characters who are inept and infirm robs them of much of their convincingness as types. The speed with which it becomes apparent that the Professor will receive no assistance from those currently in power maintains the novel's concentration on his present isolation, and to a certain extent reinforces the parallel with Thebes implied earlier. But this perfunctory treatment of the background has a further convenience for the novel, in that without completely severing the connection it distances the account somewhat from its immediate contemporary models. The aim is to stress the exemplary character of the story without entirely sacrificing its historical basis. This is most prominently the annexation of Austria (although some elements from the Spanish Civil War are blended in, most obviously the presence of a continuing left-wing resistance). The Ambassador's threats to Dr Tromp recall von Papen's bullying of the Austrian government; Grimm, the Chief of Police and covert Nazi, plays a similar role to Seyss-Inquart's; the Professor's plan for a plebiscite on national independence, though not his economic programme, invites comparison with Schuschnigg's; events both in Warner's fiction and the Anschluss turn on the dramatic developments in a radio broadcast. Warner, writing quickly and very close to the time of these events – in some cases in advance of the full revelations – had a grasp of them which has been underestimated. Katharine Hoskins thought that the Professor was presented as 'unbelievably innocent', and that the novel's political argument was weakened as a result.[6] It seems to me rather that Schuschingg, in his reckless trusting of Seyss-Inquart and Glaise von Horstenau, and in his appeal to the Western powers to make sufficiently strong representations of support for Austrian independence to deter a German invasion, while stopping short of actual intervention themselves, could be regarded as having been every bit as naive and credulous as Warner's hero, without having the latter's liberal decency and integrity – both men being placed, of course, in a situation where cunning and sophistication were hardly likely to succeed any better. It is not wholly fair for the novel to regard the Professor's willingness to stake all on a direct appeal to the electorate as self-evidently futile. Schuschnigg's planned (but never executed) plebiscite did at least have the effect of forcing Hitler into a pre-emptive strike against the possibility that it might succeed. But only in the final chapter of the novel, where the triumphant Grimm tacitly acknowledges that the Professor remains a dangerous opponent, is any further reference made to the possibility that his stance might not have been completely impractical, and that foreign sympathisers might take some action on his behalf. From the time of the Professor's first meeting with Sergeant Jinkerman, the novel deliberately presents the destiny, if not of the nation then of what the nation stands for, as depending on a direct choice between armed socialism and the Professor's disastrous refusal of it. Over and above the wider strategic analysis, however, what Warner captures so memorably from his historical model, by way of his foreshortenings and speedings-up of events, is the atmosphere of cynical manipulation, fifth-columnism, brutality and betrayal, that caused so much helpless outrage in the Western democracies at the time, and which in so many forms is more rather than less familiar today.

At the peak of his confidence, the Professor enters for the last time his favourite pastoral domains of the intellect and the senses, which, like all the realms he now moves in, are subject to alien and hostile forces. He still believes that the world of personal relationships – his intimacy with his mistress Clara – provides a bedrock of human sympathy on which a wider politics can be founded. She also supplies him with another, equally ambiguous Greek allusion:

> 'No longer, maidens with throats of hone, voices of desire, are my limbs able to bear me. Oh would that I were a kerulos who over the wave's flower flies, having a careless heart, the sea-purple spring bird.'
> 'It is lovely,' she said . . . 'is it escapism?'
> The professor kissed her parted lips and then, straightening his back, stepped past her chair and stood facing her with his hands clasped behind them. 'When I was young,' he said, 'I used sometimes to get drunk. On those occasions – there were not many of them – those words of Alcman would always come into my head. They would intoxicate me more than the alcohol, not, I think, because of their rich sensualism, the honey and the desire, but perhaps more because of the swift flashing freedom of the last lines in juxtaposition to the weight of rather vague frustration with which the poem begins. Escapism? I hardly think so. No statement so direct can be escapist.'
> 'You would like it for your epitaph, wouldn't you?' Clara said with a smile. (pp. 77–8)

This exchange is intriguingly suggestive. The portrait drawn of the Professor here is affectionately satirical; it knows that while his lecture-hall manner seems comically pedantic in this situation, it equally signifies the engagement of his deepest emotions. As usual, his main aim is to refute the implicit charge that his favourite classics have no relevance. On this occasion he attempts to discriminate the source of his feelings in the language of the fragment, in its deployment of rhythmic control over a plaintive romanticism which is less readily defended. In arguing for that kind of aesthetic sensitivity, however, he again overlooks some alternative implications of Alcman's lines. Since they almost certainly formed part of a prologue to a dance which the maidens are about to perform, and since in Spartan mythology the kerulos, or male halcyon, was supposedly carried on the back of its mate when it grew too old to fly, Alcman is expressing here not simply an old man's desire to escape the world, but a lament for his incapacity to participate in the communal activity of dancing, followed by a tacit and good-humoured recognition that he needs another's help. It is not that the Professor sentimentalises the lines; on the contrary, his effort to trace his feelings and weigh them more exactly appears, for all its pedantry, as an act of liberation in a world where emotion is manufactured or falsified at will. But he remains unable to acknowledge the extent to which, in order to effect that jubilant passage from frustration to freedom which is so expressively desired, the individual must submit to being carried by strengths other than his own. He continues proudly to assert that any compromise on his part would be too personally demeaning for him to be able to continue afterwards in pursuit of his ends – 'I could hardly ask you for your love,' he tells Clara, 'if I had deliberately failed in my duty as a human being' (p. 81). This attitude is of course unlikely to endear him to such a standardised temptress. The frankness about his principles which is intended to secure his standing in her eyes and the eyes of others always risks toppling over into the wrong kind of presumption and self-esteem.

The Professor 'escapes' with Clara to the woods for an hour, in search of a secluded spot to enhance the enjoyment of his new serenity. The narrative discloses instead that the internal problems to which the Professor remains blind are paralleled in the external world. The descriptive writing here has some curious features:

> They were looking with delight . . . at beeches whose brown buds were swollen to bursting and which were beginning now from their topmost branches to display, like flags, some few scattered and tender leaves, at the small yellow sprinkled like powder over the intricate twigs of birches and the more solid ginger of stiff-standing oaks. In the fields they observed cows careering wildly, with extended tails, along the banks of streams; and beyond the fields, in the half-dressed woods, single cherry trees flung out their brilliant and delicately loaded arms.   (p. 82)

In the middle of this slightly lush erotic display, Nature seems barely able to restrain itself from a spontaneous uprising. Leaves like flags, cows careering wildly, trees (with an effect too stunning to be deliberate) which 'flung out their brilliant and delicately loaded arms' – all insist on the impossibility of detaching any moment from the grip of contemporary pressures. One cherry tree alone seems to have achieved something like the sacred isolation of the Polis; it stands protected and aloof in its purity like an ideal version of itself, drawing the Professor like a magnet:

> For a second or two . . . they seemed to have been translated to a different mode of living, an existence that was private, ghostly, and breathless, a state between, on the one hand, the traffic-laden road and, on the other, the freshness and the melody that were fluid in the air and among the tree-tops . . . They had reached the cherry tree. Its black trunk was crowned and overbowed with a mass of snow, so that the trunk appeared like a gash or ravine in some inaccessible peak, although here what was difficult and not to be grasped was not cold, icy surfaces, rigidity or lack of air but only the unexpectedness, the fragility, and instantaneous character of what was seen. (p. 83)

The place is momentarily suspended between the dull weight of present life and the freedom of the birds above – the moment of Alcman's poem. It is a sudden glimpse in the writing of something 'difficult and not to be grasped'; the allure of a beauty which yet cannot be inhabited. In its presence the Professor feels 'bound in a new spell, his certainty of understanding and his belief in love' (p. 83). But the suspension cannot last. There are trespassers in his enchanted grove; it must dwindle back from its perfection and become a merely functional setting for a wholly contemporary pastoral debate, about 'understanding' and 'love', between the Professor's son and a girlfriend. The writing throughout this chapter seems to me simultaneously to check the excesses of the characters' sentiments and to reinforce the poignancy such checking involves; one catches in it sometimes that quiver in the voice of one whose dispassionate phrases seek to conceal his emotion.

The speech the young man makes about his position and beliefs lacks George's energetic sweep, but is both lucid and involving. The Professor's son is a figure with no distinct character to speak of, but in some respects this rather enhances than diminishes the effect of his remarks, since the gravity of the bare statement is preserved by the exclusion of extraneous personality. In his study of the 1930s novelists, *The Will To Believe*, Richard Johnstone, arguing the continuity between this version of revolutionary commitment and that in *The Wild Goose Chase*, perhaps underplayed certain differences.[7] In *The Professor* the tone is of a reluctant but firm acceptance of necessity, not a joyful embracing of a cause. Nor is there quite the impression here which obtained in George's case, that radical socialism is the one among the numerous options freely available to him that is most truly meaningful. In *The Professor* there are really no options, nor any freedom to choose. Commitment entails hatred, violence, ugliness; it entails the possibility, never entertained in the earlier novel, that one may be called upon to try to kill 'people whom I know to be better men than myself' (p. 88). The son's peroration does not entirely avoid sanctimoniousness, but leaves no room for doubt:

> We are under the terrible and necessary dictatorship of an idea. And this idea differs from many others in being entirely designed for application to the real world. It is the idea of humanity which, for a time, must submerge our own humanity. We believe that our enemies, occasionally with the best intentions, are at the moment at war with us, even if they pretend peace; and we believe that our enemies must be destroyed or else they will destroy not only us but themselves and everything that makes life dignified and promising.   (pp. 88–9)

According to this view, the Professor's liberal quest for an alternative, or even for a breathing-space in which to consider whether there are alternatives, is precisely 'escapism'. In his vanity the individual arrogates to himself a power to resist or play fast and loose with the historical moment which has chosen him. 'What does our purity or impurity matter?', the son cries; 'some petals from the cherry tree drifted slowly downwards through the air' (p. 89). There are no longer any sacred or enduringly ideal places for disinterested reflection and refreshment of the spirit. But the Professor continues to protest; his infatuation with Clara infects his rationality with a sentimental colouring. When he hears his son's girlfriend resigning herself to the view that the claims of the world are greater than those of love and love's illusory power to confer independence, the Professor, in a moment both tender and farcical, leaps to his feet and bursts through the bushes to implore the couple to go on loving, and not to waste their youth in the sterility of self-denial. The chapter closes with an image of some delicacy, when, as in the best moments of allegorical writing, the symbolic picture gathers into itself the various threads of idea and feeling that have worked their way through the developing narrative, and now touch, cross and illuminate each other:

> For a moment it seemed most surprisingly to the Professor that the sinking splendour of the sun, the scattered notes of birds, the light breeze in the branches formed together with the pain of this boy and girl a whole scene or a consistent mood, and that it was he himself, with Clara, who was standing outside the picture. The next moment the two appeared to him again as pitiful castaways, outsiders from the breathing warmth of the day. (p. 93)

In one perception the young people's condition, however ostensibly tragic, is yet fitted to and endorsed by the context which they alone have truly grasped, leaving the Professor stranded in his illusion of a timeless security. In another, that context appears as a disjunction from a larger and enduring continuity which the young cannot enter, but which the Professor, for all his present impotence, still inhabits.

The objection here is that the landscape has been simply dragooned into service by a species of pathetic fallacy. But the writing knows what costs are incurred by its decision. The moments of warmth in response to the world are signs of where the writing would wish to be, which yet do not wholly compromise its conviction that it cannot go there. Whereas in, for example, Orwell's *1984*, the 'Golden Country' is presented with full Housmanesque nostalgia and kept mysteriously clear of politicisation, Warner's pastoral retreat, with its 'loveliest of trees', answering to and challenging various perceptions of it, provides not an evasion of the problems but a complex re-encounter with them.

The rapidly accelerating momentum of the narrative now sees the Professor assailed on all sides by word and deed. There are three specific forms of attack or undermining: the anti-liberal arguments of fascism and Christianity; the further exposure of the Professor's naivety in political and personal dealings; and the socialist exhortations of his son and Sergeant Jinkerman. Warner is at his most effective in deploying a range of powerfully articulated convictions, and they are not merely set up by contrivance but arise from the action with some real dramatic force. And if, in *The Wild Goose Chase*, the threat that consciousness might be over-whelmed by the sheer quantity of material bombarding it was held off by a scepticism that still had room to operate, here is no such recourse. The Professor's increasingly numbed reactions to things suggest quite accurately the wearing-down of an overloaded mind, kept going by the spasmodic twitchings of a lifetime's habits of response when full consciousness is no longer able to reach them.

Vander, the fascist, and the elder Jinkerman, the Christian, are allegorical figures like those in the earlier novel, for whom a few brief individuating details suffice. Their histories show that neither of them conventionally typifies the position he speaks for; Vander, with his intellectual background, is not an orthodox Nazi, and Jinkerman's religious beliefs are relatively idiosyncratic. But the oblique angles from which they come at their convictions render these the more complete and fervent. Like spirits in the Inferno, who exist most intensely in their eternal reiterations of the pas-sions which govern them, these characters are so saturated by the ideas they expound as to crest into a kind of perfection beyond which there is no reaching. They both die immediately after making their speeches to the Professor, as if to emphasise the impermeable rigidity of what they have become, and the remote-ness, from the continuing world, of such foreclosed self-definitions.

Vander's fascism is both nihilistic and cynical. It envisages an élite group able to retain control over the destructive forces it unleashes, and it regards these forces as both genuine and contemptible. These are 'the dark, unsatisfied, and raging im-pulses of the real man' (p. 119), the 'vital and real forces in human nature which have so long been hypocritically oppressed by the teaching of men like you' (p. 118). According to Vander, the frustration and resentment engendered by a decaying liberal culture will be both relieved and disciplined by the state of violence which those who intend to benefit from irrationalism are deliber-ately contriving. He pours scorn on the Professor's ideals: 'Men only unite . . . when they are threatened from outside or when they have something specific to gain from someone else by force. War is a condition without which real fellow-feeling could not exist' (p. 114). (Many of these incidental points are of course dangerously close to some of the emotional satisfactions experienced by the fighting Left, whom Vander recognises to be more serious opponents than the liberal democrats; hence perhaps the stress laid in the novel, through the Professor's son, on the essentially defensive aims of the socialists.) Vander's creed is concerned with no future beyond immediate gain. It is rather a justification of the present anarchy than a programme for it, and there can be no effective refutation of his analysis other than one provided by the actual course of events in the future. But the Professor persists in treating Vander as if both men were adhering to the conventions of rational debate, and as if their opinions, however divergent and deeply-held, were adjuncts of their characters, open to comment and modification, rather than their sole substance. He is shaken by what he has heard:

> The Professor . . . was attempting to estimate, as honestly as he could, the exact force of the argument . . . He had no thought of danger, and would soon, no doubt, have begun to question the validity of the Legionary's premises and of the logical steps by which some of his conclusions had been reached. But for the moment he was speechless, for something in him which was deeper than logic had been aroused or insulted by the words of Vander. (p. 122)

But he is shaken still more by the abrupt intrusion of violence – threats, peremptory demands, shootings, blood – into what he thought of as the arena of discussion.

The turning-point of the Professor's education in how politics are really conducted comes with his attempt to broadcast to the nation. He sees this as an opportunity to use his oratorical powers to regain the initiative from those who have traduced his proposals for national independence and democratic reform. It was Clara who betrayed him, and who will do so again; his general understanding and benevolence have prevented him from penetrating to the real natures and motives of those apparently closest to him. He trusted Grimm, the Chief of Police, because of his assured and decisive bearing; the Professor never imagined such qualities being directed to dishonourable ends. He prepares for his broadcast with similar naive confidence. He imagines that the radio will provide him with the detachment and calmness so prized in his advancement of rationality:

> He ... preferred this method of oratory to any other; for, as he would often say, when the person of the speaker was invisible all inessentials and vulgarities were removed and the path of communication from mind to mind was clear.   (p. 185)

He also imagines that the only threat to the success of his speech would be ambiguous wording or hesitancy of manner on his part, which might impede the 'attractive power of a reason that permeated frontiers and dominated the interests of classes' (p. 177). This is the one occasion in the novel when the Professor attempts a thoroughgoing articulation of liberal democratic ideals, to answer in kind the speeches made against them. But his appeal is literally inaudible. Grimm cuts off the Professor's transmission, denounces him, and uses for his own ends all the resources of authority that control of the radio confers. The last of the spaces for free debate has been occupied, and Warner conjures up for the centre of his novel a magnificently simple image, of a man holding forth about liberalism into a dead microphone, imagining his audience huddled and attentive around their receivers, while in reality they are hearing something quite different.

These are the circumstances in which the Professor encounters the elder Jinkerman, and when the latter speaks, the Professor not surprisingly finds he no longer has much enthusiasm for intellectual dispute. The shock of recognising his powerlessness causes him to require more than anything what is persistently denied him, a period of calm to collect himself. Only his politeness, and 'a habit of precision rather than any real desire to convince' (p. 212), make him respond briefly in his former manner to Jinkerman. The latter represents a body of extreme Christian opinion which was regarded on the Left as having used the doctrine of original sin to arrive at a relatively comfortable accommodation with totalitarianism. Jinkerman holds liberal culture chiefly responsible for the present anarchy, and is quietly exultant over the situation, since he sees it as confirming his view that the world is perpetually constituted by suffering, and that all attempts to ameliorate man's condition by idealistic appeals are not only futile, but denials of spiritual love:

> You are alone in isolating man from man, in forcing all, friend and enemy alike, on to their own resources, in withdrawing yourself, in arrogating to yourself, a mere man, a detachment of

which only God is capable and which God, as Our Saviour has
told us, does not choose. (p. 211)

Love has nothing to do with ideals. Love is our only hold on life
and on truth. Love is what we feel for our fellow-men in misery
and in terror . . . You, in your detachment, endeavour to legislate
for the abstract man. (pp. 224–5)

In many ways Jinkerman is a more formidable opponent than
Vander. It is impossible not to be moved by what he says. His
argument has the advantage not only of its simplicity and inflexibility, but of its being sincerely informed by personal experience.
He catches the Professor at a weak moment, when the collapse of
his ambitions and his concern for his loved ones over-rides his
capacity for argument. Jinkerman exposes more acutely than
Vander had done the luxury of holding the liberal view in a world
where few can profit from it; he relentlessly points out the strict
incompatibility of such liberalism with the Christianity of which it
often claims to be a secular extension. But in the midst of his talk of
love and compassion is really a bitterness and a withering of the
spirit. It results in a passivity in some ways more appalling, in the
circumstances, than either Vander's cynical brutality or the Professor's blundering naivety. Jinkerman sees the whole potential of
mankind in the light only of his own suffering and blasted hopes,
and he welcomes the apocalypse that is about to descend, not so
much as a herald of God's ultimate triumph, but rather as a kind of
come-uppance for other people's vain pretensions, a levelling to
nullity of all human effort. The Professor is finally roused to echo
his son's speech by the cherry tree:

You may keep your purity . . . I would throw it all away if by so
doing I could save a little of that life and that confidence which
you so greatly despise. Oh, how can you be pitiful and not
indignant? The bodies are beautiful, if only for a time. (p. 235)

This moment of inner turmoil, the first irruption into the
Professor's serene rationality of passions and impulses he had
always feared and sought to restrain, is promptly matched by the
analogous turmoil of the external world. The pursuit through the
novel of this parallel, between the breaking-down of the Professor's mental security, and the taking-over by force of the old order

outside, rises here to an effective dramatic peak, where once again consciousness is forced into certain recognitions but denied the opportunity to reflect on their meaning. On this occasion the intrusion of violent reality into the arena of debate is not momentary, as with the shooting of Vander, but prolonged and overwhelming. The deafening drone of the enemy bombers pervades the room, and in a grotesque parody of a Socratic symposium the fathers and their sons are crushed together, bereft of dignity and self-control, in a confined space where their words are inaudible. 'The outer world', in which their various views were to have been acted upon, 'seemed to have become all one metallic roar' (p. 237). The Professor is now incontrovertibly faced with the completeness of his defeat, since what he stood for is no longer possible: 'Reason could hardly exist now where words had to be shouted . . . What he was seeing was the violation of a whole people, the tearing of a civilisation out of the fabric of history' (pp. 239–40).

In respect of resistance to such oppression, the sons in *The Professor* have a paradoxical advantage over their fathers. Since they do not possess selves constituted by long personal histories, the sacrifice they have to make on behalf of the struggle is of their unrealised potential, rather than the attitudes formed by their past achievements. The loss is no less bitter, but the adjustment to it is perhaps easier. The younger men recognise that it is not for them to decide the terms on which they become involved with their time; nor, although they suffer them, do they require personal catastrophes to help them make up their minds what to do. The impending war has simplified the recurrent question of how the individual is to relate to the mass; the sons seek simply to jettison their individuality and to find what fulfillment they can in impersonal collective work. Young Jinkerman always appears wearing a different disguise; over and above the need for safety is an emphatic determination not to express a self beyond the functions to which he adapts. When he first met the Professor he had urged him to realise that only the workers in arms could ever put humane ideals into practice, and that in the battle only mass movements and not individuals count for anything. But the Professor could never agree to what he would regard as a surrender of his personal independence. Even now, when the crisis of Grimm's coup has pushed the Professor further towards the socialist position, the disguise which he dons, and which enables him to witness unobserved some of the immediate consequences of the fascist triumph, is intended to see him safely back to his old life with Clara, not to enlist him in a new one.

During a brief meeting with his son the Professor had already confronted some of the emotional element in revolutionary commitment. He had attempted commiseration on the suicide of his son's girlfriend, who was raped by Vander's Legionaries (and, in anticipation of his impatience with the elder Jinkerman, the Professor had responded to this news by declaring that only practical effort was of value in a situation where 'events were taking place which no amount of theological ingenuity could possibly justify' [p. 158]). But a fastidious respect for the feelings of others, an aversion to 'obtruding' himself 'upon the secret place of another mind' (p. 147), are, for all their delicacy, part of what prevents the Professor and his son from finding a shared expression, something socially and politically cohesive. At such moments, when modern man's isolation from even his closest fellows is most starkly apparent, the Professor begins to wonder whether his classical models, which like a tragic Parson Adams he habitually consults as a first reaction to stress, can indeed provide eternal consolation. It may rather be, as the shadows of irony over his previous examples had suggested, that their true effect depends on the existence of a collective value-system, an active engagement with society not wholly consistent with the refinements of liberal humanism he was wont to infer from his favourite quotations:

> The Professor thought of the lament which Homer, in the 22nd Book of the Iliad, puts into the mouth of Andromache. Were such dignified expressions of grief, he wondered, merely the make-believe of a poet, or were they drawn from real life in societies that were differently organised from anything now existing in the world? For in modern society a sufferer ... can expect no audience to listen to his laments or to take up with him a sympathetic chorus.　　　　　　　　　　　　　　　(p. 152)

It appears now that the verbiage of party committees is the nearest equivalent, in pacifying the young man's agitation with generalities:

> It was as though this political jargon was in reality a language with a second meaning, a meaning that referred to events much closer to the heart than the meetings of agitators in crowded and

smoky rooms. The Professor could respect emotion and, in his son's words, he respected rather the echo of the individual loss than the sense of any proposal he was likely to make.   (p. 159)

In passages such as these, the initial dominant tone which the narrative had established seems to waver. The attention given to the kind of insight of which the Professor is capable runs aslant the more severe socialist view of its limitations. The reader is left to construct the implicit critique of the liberal attitude, while the narrative increasingly pursues only such aspects of the case as the Professor is able to observe. In consequence the sense of the Professor as a tragic figure undergoing a belated and painful education is emphasised at the expense of the earlier stress on his foolishness and vanity. In reacting to his son's anguish, the Professor only acknowledges the socialist position in terms of one's personal motives for holding it. He is not prepared to concede what the younger generation have tacitly argued all along, that in the present circumstances commitment to socialism is to a necessity that remains the same irrespective of their own private claims, tribulations, desires for vengeance, or even enthusiastic optimism, had they any to offer. The gap here between liberalism and socialism is as much psychological as a matter of aims and policies; the Professor's liberalism is not in any sense a discipline, which could be practised impersonally, but an attitude inseparable from the character of whoever holds it. This clash between the generations, however unsatisfactory its outcome, is conducted with a sincere mutual desire to see the best features of each other's positions, and to place the best possible construction on the rest; there is none of the mixture of paranoid petulance and self-abasement that rather disfigures the socialist attacks on liberalism in Upward's *Journey to the Border*, for example. Shock rather than argument is needed to modify the Professor's views; so long as 'no blow quite so overwhelming had ever crushed through the inner circle of fortifications that defended his own personality' (p. 153), he remained undaunted.

But when the blows do come they are the more completely overwhelming, as unlike his son he has no ready-made physical or mental retreat. As if to evoke another disquietingly tragi-comic reminiscence of Parson Adams, who, in a paroxysm of humane concern, had flung his Aeschylus into the flames, it is the sight not of cruelty or brutality but of an orgy of book-burning which really jolts the Professor:

Now he began to think of his son, of Jinkerman, and of their organisation, of which he knew so little, as the only possible defenders not only of his own safety but of the idea of humanity and of the text of Homer. (p. 268)

His own books have already been metaphorically burnt. He sees at last how little their wise passiveness about what is and will abide can assist him, since what has been lost is the vantage-point from which wise passiveness can proceed:

He thought of the passage in Lucretius in which the poet declares that from a view-point in the mountains the whole complication of an army's manoeuvres in the plain will appear simply as a stationary shimmer of light. The lines of poetry bore little reference to his actual situation. He was not on a mountain but on the outskirts of his home: and below him was a grey army which, though its individual characters were blurred in the mass, had an order and a discipline and a purpose of which he was well aware. (p. 270)

When he is captured and imprisoned in solitary confinement, he turns mechanically to the old sources of consolation, only to find to his chagrin that he cannot accurately remember the fragment of Alcman which he attempts to scratch on the stones of his cell, as if to turn it in reality into the epitaph Clara had suggested for him.

New possibilities momentarily arise from this bereavement. We come across one of those tiny spots of colour which briefly flare in the monochrome expanse, and allow glimpses into the depth of Warner's fictional world:

He heard once more the sound of footsteps in the corridor . . . He listened as though his life depended on his catching up the minutest sound, and it was with a sense almost of satisfaction that he heard what in reality he most feared, the footsteps stopping outside his door and the key turning in the lock. (p. 279)

In his moment of extremity the Professor at last experiences the concentrated singleness of being which had always previously eluded him. It has put him into a more intense and direct relationship with the world, and brought him to feel – if only for an instant – a sense of purpose stronger than what reason alone can offer, and almost in defiance of it. But since it is now too late, he can gain from it only the private satisfactions of the resister – a poor substitute for the lost possibility of effective action; behind this moment can be glimpsed the question which has haunted the liberal-humanist novel since Dickens's time and beyond, of whether and to what extent the local success can redeem or compensate for the general failure.

Shortly before his arrest the Professor had become aware that 'the terror which he had felt in the streets was being replaced by a more hostile determination which yet lacked an object' (p. 268). His new capacity to focus his undivided self upon a specific point provides him, in the midst of pain and anxiety, with a certain settled contentment. It sees him through his last interview with Grimm, who, to complete the pattern in the novel whereby all the Professor's former safeguards are dismantled, has taken into fascist hands the forms and manners of civilised debate, and now appeals to the Professor's reason and moderation. To this there can now be only one answer:

> At the moment he wished that the man could be wiped from the surface of the earth ... He thought again of his son's words 'I hate because I love' and seemed to see in the words a dreadful necessity and truth.   (p. 290)

The fetters of a liberalism which attends dispassionately to all points of view, and maintains a purity of intellect from which the emotions are excluded, are finally thrown off, and the whole personality is concentrated into a decisive commitment. It is a nice ironic touch that the last prospect the Professor should have before being murdered is of the University as seen from the prison gates – the final step on his circuitous journey towards self-recognition.

What the narrator called a 'pure kind of blindness' impeded the Professor in two ways. Not only did he not see in time the truths about current events, but a truth about himself was also hidden from him – about the role played in his commitment to rational values by elements of his being which that rationalism would rather suppress. It is appropriate that the problem should have these external and internal aspects, and that throughout the novel developments in the one should mirror those in the other, since liberalism itself always maintains a close relationship between the personal character and the abstract idea. In the socialist indictment of liberalism, that relationship is seen as mutually obstructive. Liberalism is charged with having produced damaging divisions, both in the body politic and in the self, by simultaneously nurturing certain desires and suppressing the means to realise them. The claim then is that only socialism, with its emphasis on the collective and the practical, can overcome these divisions, and put 'personal' and 'abstract' back into a properly productive partnership.

But more has been involved in this novel than the skilful illustration of a straightforward thesis. The case advanced against the liberal position can never be thoroughgoing in its condemnation so long as the sense persists, as it clearly does here, of the waste of the hero's potential rather than the revelation of his hollowness. In a more radical socialist attack, Edward Bond's for example, the contradictions of liberalism make it wholly inflexible; it could never transcend, by its mere willingness to listen, its complicity in a corrupt system which its stress on local integrity only helps to sustain. The disengaged idealism of the liberal would become an unmanageable surplus in the post-revolutionary society, because such a society would cohere only when its moral aspirations were commensurate with its practical reach. But the reader of Warner's novel senses a shift of tone. The appeal with which the book began, to the enlightened society of the future which would pass a collective judgement on the present, and on the ideas and characters which helped or hindered progress, was never fully stabilised; the intensity of the Professor's plight, and the onrush of disaster, never quite allowed for the detachment necessary to make the story consistently exemplary. In the course of its imaginative realisation of events, the novel seems to lose sight of that future relaxation, and stays instead in the present darkness, where isolated individual consciousnesses grasp what consolation they can. And as the focus changes, from the demonstration of the Professor's stupidity and unfitness, to the first hesitant steps in his conversion, it is his view of socialism, rather than socialism's view of him and of itself, that increasingly comes to take priority. As I suggested, these complications do not wholly vitiate the novel's convictions as to what is needed now. They rather add a human depth to that necessity, indicating the presence of questions that are not fully addressed; while the polemic proclaims how firmly liberalism can be damned, the form of the fiction, by concentrating and making tragic the individual's predicament, is asking how much of liberalism can be saved.

In an essay in *Les Temps Modernes* of October 1945 ('La guerre a eu lieu'), Maurice Merleau-Ponty wrote most movingly about what he called the happiness experienced by many of his comrades in the Resistance. It was the happiness of being able to feel that history had allocated them a role which yet remained personal. 'The psychological and moral elements of political action were almost the only ones to appear here ... This experience broke away from the famous dilemma of being and doing, which confronts all intellectuals in the face of action'.[8] It seemed that the simple fact of the Nazi takeover had created a moment when the doctrinal conflicts between liberalism and socialism were overborne, and the only conviction that mattered was that the actions one took were both indisputably right and privately satisfying. This was the point where it appeared that one's individual significance was not being sacrificed to necessity, but expressed in it. No doubt a great deal of disillusionment subsequently arose from the understandable desire of the survivors to carry over into different circumstances an elation such as this, which was shaped by, and inextricably belonged to, the specific conditions of clandestine or open resistance. In *The Professor* the crisis is too close for such further concerns to register other than faintly. In *The Aerodrome* Warner will reopen some of the routes that are here temporarily cordoned off.

Notes

1. Samuel Hynes, *The Auden Generation*, pp. 227–8.
2. Rex Warner, 'The Uses of Allegory', in *Penguin New Writing* no. 17, 1943, p. 140.
3. Arnold Rattenbury, introduction to *The Professor* (Lawrence & Wishart reprint, 1986), p. 5.
4. Katharine Bail Hoskins, *Today the Struggle*, University of Texas Press, 1969, p. 138.
5. Hynes, p. 314.
6. Hoskins, p. 138.
7. Richard Johnstone, *The Will To Believe*, Oxford 1982, pp. 56–7.
8. Maurice Merleau-Ponty, 'La guerre a eu lieu'; translated as 'The War has taken place' in *Sense and Non-Sense*, trans. Hubert and Patricia Dreyfus, Northwestern University Press, 1964, p. 151.

4

The Aerodrome

The titles of Warner's previous novels had identified their themes more or less directly; one suggested a journey of uncertain outcome, the other the predicament faced by a particular type of individual. For the third book the emphasis is on place, and since this particular aerodrome occupies an elevated position, it may appear to be the place to which both the journey and the predicament have been leading – a shining city on a hill, where all uncertainties are dispelled. T. E. Lawrence told Robert Graves that joining the Air Force was 'the nearest modern equivalent of going into a monastery in the Middle Ages'[1]; it is one that commits its members, however, to the active as well as to the contemplative life. Those who live at the aerodrome in Warner's novel certainly seem to comprise an élite group, set apart from the common world, pure and unswerving in their dedication to the perfect accomplishment of their allotted tasks. They are secured, by their interdependent positions within a hierarchy, from the anxieties of alienation. Each airman, lowly or exalted, has a role in the smooth operation of systems and rituals to whose fuller significance only a select few are privy; and just as the monastic kitchens did their best to compensate the flesh for its privations, so at the aerodrome the harsh regime is punctuated by bouts of epicurean pleasure.

Although flight is the principal objective, the attractive glamour of the air force that Warner presents is not just confined to those with ambitions to be pilots. It derives as much from the simpler desire to be incorporated within a fully-fledged, uniformed organisation, whose conditions and rewards apply at least in some measure to all ranks. Indeed the romance of the solo flyer, for some years the source of a twentieth-century hero cult, was already rather fading by the time of *The Aerodrome*, which was written in the summer of 1939 – although not published until 1941, by which time of course the Battle of Britain had temporarily revived certain sentiments. The Nietzschean figure that Yeats imagined and Auden adopted, driven by 'a lonely impulse of delight' to an austere aloofness from the common squabble, seems already rather to belong to a pioneering past of accident and adventure. The helmeted airman had been unique among the combatants on the Western Front, in his freedom from trammelling conditions and in the almost chivalrous directness of his contact with the enemy; in the post-war years he (and she) had been able to undertake ever more arduous and exotic journeys. By now, however, advances in technology and administration are beginning to rein in some of that individuality and compass the pilot round with any number of invisible supports; Roy, the youthful narrator of Warner's novel,

> used to listen with a kind of regret to the stories told to us by our instructor . . . of crashes caused by faulty construction that today would be impossible; of fights with storm and snow of which the pilot had not been forewarned; of how it had even been necessary to employ strength in handling the controls. He would look at us somewhat sadly . . . and say: 'A kite used to take some flying in those days' . . . For whatever we attempted in the air we could be certain at all times that our machines would respond with absolute accuracy to the controls, and there was consequently no danger whatever except for those who were either physically or mentally in any case unfit for flying.   (p. 190)

It is characteristic that Roy's generation should feel both more and less favoured than their fathers, who are shown in the novel to have started as enthusiastic mountaineers before progressing through the earliest days of powered flight to their present degree of mastery. The relationship between man and machine which *The Aerodrome* so variously explores is encountered by the younger men at a point of precarious balance. The reduced level of uncertainty – 'no danger whatever' – provokes both satisfaction and regret, and the faith that is placed in the precise responses of man-made creations may lead to difficulties unknown amid the hardships of the cloister.

Of all Warner's novels, *The Aerodrome* is the one with the most obvious superficial resemblances to Kafka. But even here, the mysterious centre of authority on a hilltop dominating a village, and the hero's relationship with a barmaid of uncertain allegiance, seem almost unconscious borrowings. Warner himself, in a *Guardian* interview in 1974, recalled how his novel had its origin in the grumblings he overheard, among the regulars at a Cotswold pub, about the incessant noise of aircraft overhead.[2] It is clearly the most personal of his writings; he chooses a narrator with a name similar to his own, and draws on scenes and customs familiar from his country-rectory boyhood, juxtaposing them with their modern counterparts in order to offer, in metaphorical and allegorical form, a retrospective assessment of his generation's political and psychological history. The atmosphere of the writing also reflects the now-unavoidable fact of the imminent war, and its impact upon personal or collective ambitions. When one's projects for the future may at any moment be cut off or transformed beyond recognition, there is an oscillation, between seizing for oneself whatever chance of control is offered, and a more passive and limited trust in the falling-out of things. What has gone is the note of exhortation, heard in the earlier novels, to urgent and decisive action on the basis of what can be shown to be held in common. In place of that turbulent energy is a self-absorption, an inward communing that never issues in a concrete programme, a heightened and protective concern with immediate personal balance and safety.

The Aerodrome accordingly makes different use of those basic elements from the earlier novels which it reconvenes. Like *The Professor* it deals with the takeover by totalitarian forces of an old order in decay; like *The Wild Goose Chase* its narrative is organised by the hero's movements between two worlds, rural and futuristic. But the nature of the takeover, the character and role of the hero, and the relationship between the different environments, are substantially changed. The novel's setting is this time unequivocally English, in deep country remote from the centres of power, yet bound to them by traditional patterns and continuities; Roy, the village's expectancy and rose, is intended for the Civil Service. The building of an aerodrome on a nearby hill, and its rights of occupation and redesignation of local land and labour use, are legitimately authorised by the distant government which the members of the village hierarchy unquestioningly respect. Hence, although a few violent incidents precede and accompany it, the occupation when it comes is relatively calm. There is no coherent opposition, nor need for any coercive display of the military might which the village is now expected to service. In place of the explosive upheavals and bursts of aggression in *The Professor* is an almost dreamy and bemused submission to the inevitable; the village seems to drift into a transformation whereby familiar outlines are retained and modified rather than demolished. Nor do the villagers' attitudes towards the powers that control them neatly divide, as in *The Wild Goose Chase*, between dulled peasant subjection and clandestine revolt. There are instead feelings of greater complexity, ranging from vague resentment and grudging acceptance to more or less overt admiration and envy, and often incorporating elements of all of these. Political ideas and issues rarely announce themselves as directly here as in the other books. *The Aerodrome* examines the edges rather than the centre of the contemporary crisis – or rather, it represents a move to the periphery in search of an alternative view of the centre. By now there is no longer any prospect of a revolution overthrowing fascism and its allies, and Warner's always brittle confidence that it would successfully do so seems to have left him. If the enemy is to be defeated it will have to be by the 'free world' as it is, and not as socialism would wish it to be. The confrontation, moreover, is not just with a power against which certain military and political strategies and alliances are in order; it is increasingly with an attitude that stirs and attracts even those threatened by it. *The Aerodrome* explores in microcosm a social psychology not unlike that identified by Fromm and Dewey and other commentators upon the appeal of totalitarianism and its latent presence in the democracies; the simplicity and resonance of many of the novel's images raise in addition questions that belong more generally to other encounters with the modernising spirit, of which Warner's Air Force is an extreme case.

The taking-over, or absorption, of the old by the new, is registered internally in the narrator's mind as well as externally in the world. Roy, who tells his own story, is unlike Warner's other youthful characters in his lack of interest in politics. His account demonstrates how certain tendencies of mood and taste, and the impressions made on him by other people, acquire a political cast almost unconsciously. The links between him and the older generation are not broken by rebellious self-assertion on his part, as with George; nor by the intervention of history, as with the Professor's son. There is instead a series of revelations as to how those links were forged through fraud and deception from the beginning, and Roy is rather appalled than radicalised by being thus set adrift. He is certainly not prompted to adopt an urgent cause, nor to put aside his immediate desires in favour of higher things. On the contrary, he finds some aspects of the loss of his former life quite agreeable. It enables him to concentrate such languid energies as he has upon first love, for example, which

Warner presents attractively and without strain: 'I thought of my love surrounding her like a cloak and of her walking forward sweet and unconscious of it' (p. 113). Such a thought could apply to much of Roy's own experience; he too moves with nonchalance among shaping and accompanying forces of whose presence he only gradually becomes aware. As a first-person narrator, he reassembles and reflects upon his experience, offering his maturer self as a means of interpreting and drawing conclusions from the past. But for all his honest efforts to put things into order, his narrative is studded with moments of involuntary self-betrayal, and registers only the vaguest consciousness on his part of whole areas of significance and connection traced in the writing, which his reader alone can detect. Even at the zenith of his Air Force career, as secretary to the Air Vice-Marshal, he never becomes a convincing exponent of the abstract ideas he is employed to help realise. We always remember that he enlisted at the aerodrome for mixed reasons, and the contentment he finds there derives as much from his youthful buoyancy as from coherent or settled beliefs. The very ordinariness of Roy, ordinariness that never ceases to be so amid all the extensions and transformations it is caught up in, helps empty his experience of any grating particular-ities and allows the reader the more readily to fill it with his own equivalents. Roy's imprecise contact with conflicting creeds, his awareness that things are wrong coupled with his wish to control the extent to which that awareness impinges on him, his blindness to much of what he pronounces upon, appear as more 'realistic' indices of what it might actually have been like to grow up at that time than do the more bravely committed or persistently self-conscious heroes encountered elsewhere. The opening-out from the commonplace to the large and general is done in my view modestly and without undue pretentiousness; understated and often humorous typicality is an important part of the novel's success. For Anthony Burgess it produces 'a comedy of high seriousness',[3] while Angus Wilson went so far as to say that Roy's is 'the history of every socially, morally conscious liberal minded man in those decades between the wars'.[4]

Roy is never of course a mere cipher of these things; he is also selfish, priggish and cruel. And an additional reason, perhaps, why his experience could be so promptly and widely recognised and viewed with sympathy may be that he is never actually called on to commit evil – although he does condone the evil of others, in a language of bureaucratic euphemism which is shown to be acquired with chilling ease. The wider consequences of fascist domination are suggested rather than displayed. But to localise the power, as *The Aerodrome* does, and to project it as ultimately collapsing under the weight of its inner contradictions, is not to trivialise or under-estimate its threat. The novel is more concerned with the genesis of totalitarian attitudes than with the details of what people do who hold them. The attitudes themselves moreover never settle into an orthodox fascist mould which could be regarded as safely alien, belonging to a different order of experience which may threaten but not seduce our own; the insistence here is on something at once more familiar and more uncomfortable that may underlie a number of alternative political programmes. The creed which the Air Vice-Marshal puts forward is quite different from Vander's in *The Professor*. The emphasis is no longer on violence and blood-instinct, the vengeful rising-up of the servile against their idealistic oppressors. The Air Vice-Marshal's doctrine is of self-mastery as a precondition for mastery of others, of liberation of the mind from the fetters of convention, instinct and blood-ties, and of the rebuilding, along wholly rational lines, of the self in the image of the Leader. There is a Stalinist element in this forcible purging and reconstruction; the aerodrome seems in part a refuge not for anarchy and resentment but for a ruthless and hardened radical idealism, close to the more rhetorical forms that George's had taken. When, near the end of the novel, the Air Vice-Marshal talks disparagingly of the 'low aims' of traditional village life (p. 295), his phrase echoes George's commendation of what he called Shake-speare's 'undeviating contempt' for those with merely 'low aims' (*WGC*, p. 186). Warner here traces through some of the less palatable consequences of his youthful Marxist rebelliousness shorn of its benevolent motives. But the Air Vice-Marshal is much closer overall to Nazism in his cultivation of the Ubermensch, the new breed or superior race who combine their grand conceptions with a seem-ingly unstoppable military power and strictness, seeking to rid the world of its impurities in order to make living space for themselves:

> We constituted no revolutionary party actuated by humane ideals, but seemed to be an organisation manifestly entitled by its own discipline, efficiency, and will to assume supreme power. Outside us I could see nothing that was not incompetent or corrupt.   (p. 226)

This organisation is more concerned to answer to the desires of those who join it than to address itself to the needs of those elsewhere. It is no foreign power out to conquer and enslave the natives, but a form in their midst to which their own self-centred and arrogant dissatisfactions can be adapted.

Such proximity, such localisation of the issues within an enclave, is reinforced by the novel's adoption for allegorical purposes of the form of country-house melodrama, where a range of types is gathered into a confined area. The conventional world it draws on, of rectors, squires, butlers, gardeners, maids, strange visitors and revenants from the past, is an unforced literary mutation of the actual world of Warner's youth; it is full of apparently random shocks which actually rest upon a buried chain of causes and consequences. The techniques of such melodrama are suited to the political enquiries of *The Aerodrome*, because they concern themselves with the hidden relationships between ostensibly separate things, the mystery of origins and legacies. There is no independent detective-figure piercing the veils that custom, error and deliberate imposture throw over the truth; there is rather a working-through of a daemon which exhausts its complicated family. As the revelations which occur in the course of this process are partial or misleading, the hero's education into reality is more haphazard and accidental than that of the heroes of allegorical quests, who can be sustained amidst all their trials by a steady vision of their goal. In *The Aerodrome*, moreover, the erratic unfolding of the plot is not designed to result in a solution which merely disposes of the obscurities for good, but to demonstrate the previously unrecognised extent and continuity of the entanglements from which Roy has vainly tried to free himself. Variants of the country-house genre were common among the Auden group's earlier writings, but Warner no longer uses his stock types for the immediate rewards of farce or satire. He endows them with the kind of seriousness and capacity for sympathy essential to true comedy, so that their life always provokes in Roy an ambivalent response from which love and affection are never extirpated, even at the height of his disgust. There is a sense in the novel of how the very weight and encrustation of habit, etiquette and tradition in the old order produce an inertia, a built-in resistance to the most confident and aggressive efforts to expose its failings to the brutal light of reason, and this intangible code comes to elicit as much respect from Roy as exasperation. The adolescent urge to get clean away from it all is now itself a primary subject of investigation – a considerable change from the implicit approval, in *The Wild Goose Chase*, of George's violent and symbolic rejection of the environment that fostered him, in a spectacular rupturing of provincial ceremonies. While at times, particularly during the scenes of Bess's illness, the machinery of the melodrama rather audibly creaks, for the most part it provides the novel with an unobtrusive framework whose own complexity is skilfully disguised.

The enduring interest of the book has for me only partly to do with the 'prophetic qualities' Burgess mentions,[5] or the immediate relevance of its main subject. *The Aerodrome* has little of the sensational impact of other dystopias of the time with which it tends to be compared, nor does it produce inventions and neologisms that enter the currency and outlive the books they adorned. It offers instead a number of images and impressions that can lodge in the mind more quietly, to emerge whenever, as G. W. Stonier wrote in 1945, 'we catch the new supplanting the old: a factory in a valley, a block of flats ousting a slum'.[6] We are given glimpses of states in transition graphically juxtaposed, or of the retention in new usages of old conditions – the airfield buildings camouflaged to appear natural; Roy and his fellow pilots watching a display of remote-controlled flying; the underground chapel with its plush seats resting on the bare rock; the manor house converted to a country club; the young villagers inspecting the latest farm machinery alongside stalls selling basketwork and rush-plait dog leads. Each simple and momentary catching-sight of the world assists in the broadening of the vision, until the novel becomes the expression of a much larger subject than is overtly described. Some of those images are deliberately created, some casually observed at large; all help to identify as the principal theme the conflicting responses provoked by change and displacement, the struggle between life and the forms in which it settles. Nor is *The Aerodrome* merely *about* such conflicts; they are enacted in the procedures of the writing.

Roy is discovered lying face down in black mud at the bottom of a meadow. The mud 'smelt good'; he turns his cheek to its caress, opening a panorama of trees, stars and darkness which swells the intoxication to which he has already partially surrendered. For a moment he gives way to romantic indulgence: the trees are 'like giants guarding beneficently the field of a dream' (p. 13). Shortly afterwards the snarl of an owl will reinvigorate his nature-worship: 'it was as though my very bowels were pierced with a sudden excitement, like a lancet, of joy' (p. 14). But already this thick mouthful has been bitten back. The 'spaces' between his fingers, where the mud oozes so sensually, become the 'interstices' of his 'hard dress shirt', 'penetrated' by the 'point of a long reed' (p. 13). Since mud and reeds have a considerable part to play in what follows, the registration on the first page of Roy's mingled pleasure and discomfort with them is not arbitrary; nor are the rhythms of his oscillation, which the mud and the reeds help to define, between letting go and drawing back. The language suggests a newly-born creature emerging from the earth as from an amniotic sac, or suddenly aroused by sexual contact into a guilty recoil; the pedantic precision of 'interstices' quickly throws a hygienic screen over the slimy mess. It sets going a continuous allegorical accompaniment to Roy's own more heedless observations; my commentary will touch only lightly on it while following Roy's progress, and aim to gather the threads later. Roy's Fall is itself actually the result of blundering into a tripwire – an unexpected contact with the hidden frontiers of a field he had imagined safe and clearly marked. Meanwhile the trees, its ostensible guardians, which are indistinguishably 'dim shapes' at the moment, are available in daylight for a more exact taxonomy:

> In the churchyard there is one tall tree, a libocedrus, which runs up into the air like a black flame, and which, when I was a boy, I used to worship, visiting it regularly after morning service, thrusting my head and hands through its dark foliage, fancying it to be some goddess or divine creature, not uninterested in myself. Though embedded in earth it seemed a visitor from another world, like the people at the aerodrome, for it was the only conifer in the churchyard and stood most purely among the gigantic horse-chestnuts whose sticky huge buds were now peeling into leaf. (pp. 15–16)

The Professor also had a special tree, but it quickly proved by losing its blossoms to be no more privileged than the others. Here, however, the boy with the taste for scientific names is engaged by the mysterious alien, which shares the same foundation as common trees but stands apart from them, with its black, flame-like purity among the sticky, peeling world of ordinary nature. It seems

graciously to entice the neophyte away from his merely conventional church rituals into dreams of shared importance and superiority, of a state fully-formed and immune from the cumbersome
and messy procedures of growth. The 'people at the aerodrome'
are rapidly associated with a new, or rather a returned Nature; an
Olympian visitation which unites in its proud dark straightness
pastoral nostalgia and adolescent male ambition for sexual power
and its associated re-orderings of the world. Such people are
figured too in the precise aloofness of 'libocedrus', the Oregon
incense cedar, that must so easily dominate the church, with its
'short square tower', and the Manor, with its mere 'cedar' tree and
'well-kept lawn'. Roy's earliest sanctuary, the unkempt Rectory
garden, has the consolations of familiarity; he knows 'the smell of
leaves and grass in rain and sunshine; the consistency and colour
of the soil in different parts' (p. 16). But the cosiness of it all is
implicitly challenged by this fascinating new arrival; art seems here
to have been used not just to imitate Nature, but to recover, in a
manner Pope might have admired, the mysteries which are
elsewhere tamed:

> The long hangars were set not in rows nor in any regular order,
> but were so disposed and camouflaged that even from quite
> close at hand they appeared merely as rather curious modifica-
> tions of the natural contours of our hills. The living quarters for
> officers and men were equally well hidden, some in natural
> indentations of the ground, others in thick groves of evergreen
> trees which had been specially planted for the purpose. Many of
> the buildings also, where visible, resembled older landmarks.
>   (p. 17)

Roy has not yet crossed the other frontier, the main road that
separates the aerodrome from the village. But just as his drunken
meander through the muddy field is promptly arrested by the
tripwire, so the thoughtlessly secure identity he once possessed
has been sent sprawling by the Rector's revelation that Roy's true
parentage and origins are unknown; that he was found 'at about
the place where the main road now is' (p. 25), and that he has now
to regard himself not as a known dweller in a known village but as
an alien surrounded by a conspiracy of secrets:

> Now I turned my eyes again to the shadowy elm trees, darker

than the sky, and they seemed no longer kindly, but like dreadful moving pillars, forcing me from my place. For these hills and woods and meadows were not mine as I had thought them, nor was I myself what I had been brought up to think myself to be. (p. 19)

What appeared to be smooth and natural was, on closer inspection, actually constructed by cunning deceptions; the foundling's story is a 'rather curious modification' of the legitimate child's. But in this case there seems no pleasure or utility in the rearrangement; at the intersection of mud and wire the cosiness is not only challenged but dispelled, and the aerodrome seeps into consciousness as a clean and austere improvement upon a hopelessly flawed and degraded original. When the Flight-Lieutenant, Roy's friend from the aerodrome who attends the birthday celebration, challenges the Rector about his story, he does so in the authentic ringing voice of the inter-war generation: 'It is a fact, is it not, that for the last twenty-one years you have been telling lies? May I ask what is your authority for this?' (p. 26). (This dates the origin of the deception back to 1918, incidentally.) The Rector has his reply ready and equally resounding:

"If you want my authority for the care I have taken of him, it is love, sir, justice, sir, and pity." (p. 26)

Roy has suddenly found himself to be the object, not of familiar regard, but of vast abstractions, as if a divine creature has indeed shown interest in him. He staggers out into the dark towards the meadow, overcome by a confusion more extreme than his style now will permit: 'not that I felt anything but gratitude to my benefactors, but merely that I lacked assurance' (p. 27). Uncertain of his emotions, uncertain of his identity, Roy is pushed inexorably towards a similar role to that of the 'surveyor' established in Auden's *Journal of an Airman*. From this vantage he will recover a different security, in which the excitements of discovery will always be honed into practical benefit; there may still be surrenders to the moment, but they will have their controlled place, and prime objectives will not be forgotten. So 'spaces' turn to 'interstices'; an incense cedar is a 'libocedrus'; the precision and the detachment which align him in spirit with the aerodrome already are all part of a joyous discipline, a burnishing of things – 'si canimus silvas, silvae sint consule dignae'.[7]

The surveyor's mode of seeing, his concern to be exact and disengaged even in intimacy, is of course at constant risk from the prospects it yields. Something is always likely to slip or ooze through the fingers which search for a secure and orderly grasp, or to escape the eyes which patrol the perimeter fences. While we encounter Roy's cautious reconstruction of the process whereby he comes to confront the allegory in which he so heavily figures, we encounter also the stumblings, the frontiers, the limits of pattern or formal organisations that aim to mediate between the subject and his experience. The new breed of airman has transformed the old symbol of flight; the desire to escape, with the wild goose or the kerulos, from the constraints of the human element, is now a desire to master it; the pilot with his bombs and his hawk's eye has a new force and a new perspective. Roy's story, of becoming an airman and his subsequent recusancy, is itself a continuous flight, from complexity to simplicity and back again; it is a pastoral movement which is never resolved, as the local forms of the writing and the circumscribing allegory both represent further and persistent ambitions for certainty and control, even after these seem to have been ceremoniously abandoned by the character himself. The novel does not just consider and explode the attractions of fascism. It considers also a willingness to be attracted which is still in pursuit of its ends, a desire not wholly vanquished by disappointment.

One consequence of Roy's fall into a corrupt and more complex world is a new capacity, which he repeatedly mentions, to experience conflicting emotions simultaneously. The novel is subtitled 'a love story', and its narrator discovers love and aversion, attraction and repulsion, sympathy and distaste, coexisting not just in the dark marsh but everywhere he turns. The insights he is offered into the furious and destructive passions which rage beneath the restraints of village life, passions in which his own identity is mysteriously implicated, cause him to drift ever more uneasily between states of momentary astonishment and numb curiosity. Meanwhile the allure of the aerodrome, as a harbour where these divergences might be safely gathered in, gains strength from the terms in which Roy expresses his difficulties:

What I had thought to be solid, rounded, and entire, now seemed to melt into frightful shapes of mist, to dissolve into intricacies wherein I was lost as though I had never been.
(pp. 123–4)

Nothing more 'solid, rounded, and entire' than an aircraft hangar, that modified contour of the now-strange hills, 'curved in a way so like the natural roundness of this land, and yet in its perfect regularity so unlike' (p. 104). Nestling against that ideal breast one might find safety from passions, embarrassments, the unsuspected weaknesses in things taken for granted, and all the irritating and problematic demands they seem to make upon diffuse responses.

While attending the village Agricultural Show Roy witnesses the mawkish and comical lament of a drunken grocer, who affirms for his audience that 'love', for the 'old place', and for the mother who sits 'poking the fire, thinking, ah thinking, of your wandering son' (p. 61), occupies the one clean corner of his otherwise rotten heart. The grocer clings to the habit of this performance just as the villagers cling to the habit of listening; the rules that govern the game of sentiment are too well known on both sides for any contact with genuine feeling to survive. Roy recounts this episode, and that of the human rat-catcher which follows, with a complete absence of involvement. Sentimentality and mindless cruelty are alike accepted village mores, wholly severed from what origin they might have had in experience; what Roy later calls the 'cohesion of our village' (p. 76) appears largely as the collective deadening of the senses by the weight of local tradition. One of the threats posed by the aerodrome to that cohesion comes from its encouraging the spontaneous expression of urges which in the village are constrained or vicarious. An airman hits a villager in the face with a broken glass, instead of abiding by the time-honoured conventions of bar-room combat; the Flight-Lieutenant turns loose a prize bull, 'in direct contravention of the rules that govern the life of villages' (p. 57). But envy of such daring quickly mingles with the villagers' indignation: 'before very long people began to laugh rather than grumble at what had happened' (p. 57), since such incidents seem to result from a licence to convert desire into action, a briskness and efficiency that stirs up some of the impulses so long silted and forgotten in timorousness and deference. In Roy's case, these early stages of the relationship between village and aerodrome produce a nice touch of comedy, of which he, as usual, seems not wholly aware. Having used his skill to win a haul of coconuts from the shy, he wanders off with his girlfriend Bess past a stall where the Flight-Lieutenant is demonstrating the latest machine-guns. Bess smiles wistfully across at the officer while Roy grapples with his absurd luggage: 'I pressed the coconuts hard against my side, extending my fingers so as to cover as much as possible of their surfaces' (p. 67).

By the time it is discovered that the Flight-Lieutenant had accidentally loaded live ammunition, with which he has killed the Rector, Roy's already imprecise grip on his emotions has been further relaxed by his first sexual adventure with Bess. His feelings are expressed simply, in language which says nothing new but everything right:

> I could not think of her as of a person like myself, but rather as a sudden glow on water or something exquisite and airy and apt to move away, like a bird or a cloud's shadow sweeping across a wood. Thus there was fear and perturbation in my intense happiness. (p. 46–7)

It is a version, touching in its naivety, of the dream Florizel had of Perdita, the anxiety to hold on to something that fascinates by its movement; that it should 'move still, still so, and own no other motion'. Roy is also aware that his desire for Bess has an additional target, recalling the libocedrus: 'when our eyes met, there would be a mistiness in her gaze, a withdrawal into some other world that attracted me, but attracted me to something other than herself' (p. 65). Contact with such mist ('frightful' later, but alluring now) ought to gain him access to a state in which the tawdriness that surrounds him will be shut out – but shut out somehow more valuably than by the mere blankness into which he habitually retreats: 'as I stared into her eyes, the river, the meadow, the hare, and the rooks seemed to recede from me as the whole Agricultural Show had already receded' (p. 68). But their sexual performance is 'loose and scrambling', and it fails to transfigure them. Roy 'was surprised to see her face not changed, but much more ordinary than it had been before ... I began to feel that, in spite of what I was impelled to say, nothing very remarkable had taken place' (pp. 68–9). Events do not seem to match expectations; the ideal seems to slip from grasp at the moment of capture. Imperfect fulfillment provokes Roy to further desire, but he is unable to communicate this feeling to Bess and is left more confused than before: 'I felt, together with a wave of tenderness, a sharp pang of exasperation and almost of contempt for her' (p. 69). Everywhere in the village the impelling passions are staled by custom or complicated by what they touch; and meanwhile the Flight-Lieutenant, together with all he symbolises of the force behind him, continually appears on the margins of the scenes of Roy's growing pains.

The latest perplexing discovery is the Rector's body, the image of a life whose once clear and separate pieces now congeal in an indistinguishable mess. Roy approaches it with affection and recoils from it in horror, so far short it falls of representing the well-organised system the Rector's existence seemed to have. (The Rector's confession to a murder, which Roy overheard, had also cracked the façade, but rather by replacing one system with another.)

> It would have been better, perhaps, if the Rector's features had been left intact. Some effect of dignity or of the statuesque might then have been achieved. As it was it was only the pulp of a man that lay under the white sheet, unrecognisable except to those who possessed special knowledge.   (p. 71)

The emotional life of the village is rather like that; it leaves the white sheet of convention and blankness to stand for a dignified serenity which the pulp beneath does not actually have. The aerodrome's bullets have revealed that inchoate mass as much as caused it; the Rector's remains are so different from the village's perception of him, and by extension of itself, as to seem 'more a trophy of an abstract power than a reminder of the living' (p. 72). The aerodrome has by now been associated with nature, love, and death, well before we actually visit it. As for 'special knowledge', the kind arising from private and tender remembrances of friendship has ceded ground to another, the ruthless public inspection of brute details which were previously covered up. Increasingly Roy finds himself inclining towards this latter. When he learns from the Squire that the Air Force intends to take over the entire village, Roy's response to the old man's defeat brings his paradoxical emotions fully to consciousness:

> There was such sincerity in his words, he seemed so abject in his courtesy, that I longed for some power of speech or gesture that would enable me to show him affection that was more than pity. But this feeling, however warm, was momentary. I seemed to see in his shrunken face and in the lines that constricted his temples something already dead which reminded me of the really dead body of the Rector lying still in the upper room. And

against this I reacted with aversion so strong that I felt hypocritical as I pressed his hand and urged him to make use of me in
any way that he could do so. I hope that he recognised the love
and did not notice the aversion. Both feelings were genuine and
both spontaneous.   (pp. 82–3)

There is a recurrent uneasiness in Roy's style when he finds
himself in the grip of the spontaneous while yearning for control
and clarity; a tautness about the over-precise descriptions which
speaks of a concern to bear accurate witness to something under
imminent threat of encroachment or loss. There is another brief
sign of this the following morning, when he describes the familiar
sounds of the village in a staccato series, too rapid and fragmented
to be truly comforting. It is immediately after this that the Air Vice-
Marshal arrives for the Rector's funeral. The newcomer promptly
arouses the same combination of responses as the Squire, for
exactly opposite reasons: 'I disliked the complete assurance of his
look, but at the same time felt attracted to the apparent power and
confidence of the man' (p. 88). Not only does he stand in straightforward opposition to the Squire and the late Rector; he seems also
to reinvigorate modes of behaviour which, for them, had ceased to
express real self-control but had become lacklustre and routine. All
the Air Vice-Marshal's 'movements seemed to be made unwillingly,
and yet with perfect dignity and precision' (p. 88). Roy is disgusted
by the excitement aroused among the mourners by this stranger
who shows no reverence, and troubled also by hints of his own
complicity; all the sounds and patterns of his former life seem to
fade with the funeral bell, 'like one of those strange silences that
one notices in the summer, sitting in the woods, perhaps, when
the birds suddenly stop singing and the sound of insects dies away
and one strains one's ears after what is inaudible' (p. 93). The Air
Vice-Marshal strides ruthlessly into that silence, mounts the pulpit, and cuts open all the conventions the villagers rely on to
conceal from themselves their uncertainty and hypocrisy:

'The man is dead. His family is, I believe, well provided for.
That, on this subject, is all, I think, which needs to be said.'
    Here he paused and I felt, as I am sure a greater part of the
congregation felt, a kind of impotent rage at the inhumanity of
the words which we had heard . . . the thought flashed through
my mind of making some protest against what had been said;

but to do any such thing would have seemed to disturb the peace and dignity of the dead ... 'I have made these preliminary remarks,' he said, 'because it is customary at a funeral to make some mention of the dead man. But I would have you know that what is customary among you – sentimentality, mawkishness, and extravagant praise of those who are already sufficiently well-known – is considered amongst us of the Air Force neither customary nor proper.' (pp. 95–7)

Roy rather congratulates himself on his restraint here, but what he calls 'inhumanity' is really the clear, public expression of what he had vaguely and fearfully felt to be true; no rage is so impotent as that which cannot find a stable target. His responses swirl among the various forms the villagers' take, from the spluttering resentment of an elderly man promptly forced from the building by two Air Force officers, to the 'dumb and ox-like' curiosity (p. 96) of the rest, as he longs for some means of access to the power that provokes him:

Though I knew the people here well, and loved them, I was disgusted and frightened by the contrast between their quick anger, their sudden levity, and the undeviating precision and resolution of the Air Vice-Marshal. I longed for the time when the bar would close and I could put my arms round Bess, for I fancied that in her love there was some security. (p. 103)

His desire, which Bess continues to arouse by withholding full satisfaction, involves a movement away from village conventions towards the other world, of the undeviating and the precise, like the libocedrus he also sought to embrace. He certainly wishes that his feelings were shared and understood by someone 'not unin-terested' in himself, and thereby clarified into an order that would banish his anxiety. It is Bess, who hitherto has said very little, and nothing to suggest she has a life independent of Roy's imagination of it, who unwittingly and tactlessly puts her finger on the wound he cannot bring himself to acknowledge openly:

Her first words to me were: 'Wasn't he marvellous?' and, when I enquired of whom she was speaking, she said it was the Air Vice-Marshal, and then paused, embarrassed perhaps because it had occurred to her that she had said something to offend me, as indeed she had. (p. 104–5)

His eagerness to rid himself of these contradictions is stronger, however, than his hurt vanity, and when Bess goes on to propose that he join the Air Force, he agrees. His principal rationale for so doing is that it would facilitate a rapid secret marriage, which he imagines would both express his new liberty and put his relationship with Bess on to the secure and permanent footing he desires. He would then be free to enjoy his immediate pleasures untrammelled by 'the obligations, the conventions, the manners' in which he had been brought up (p. 109). Roy shows no awareness of the wider significance of his decision, nor of the kind of ideological commitment it will entail. On the contrary, he regards the aerodrome at this point merely as a convenience whose modern and streamlined efficiency can be made use of, while he reserves for himself the right to dissent from or limit the conditions imposed on him in return. There is a genuine pathos, I think, about Roy's mood in these scenes; the drift towards the totalitarian vision is shown as so simply prompted by the displacement of identity from its home, and its apparent relocation in the projections of private feeling, of a kind that looks back to Hardy and beyond: 'Having lost the security in which I had been bred, I now looked at Bess, weak and childish as she was, as at a new and certain world' (p. 108). And again, scarcely are these hopes of compensation brought to mind than the Flight-Lieutenant reappears, as if the aerodrome formed a kind of growth or accretion upon Roy's emotional life that spreads steadily and unnoticed over it.

In Roy's recollection of the extent of his self-absorption in love is a note reminiscent of Auden's 'Lay your sleeping head':

> If unreflecting happiness, indifference to the outside world, a sudden and prolonged delight in the pleasures of the senses are characteristic of honeymoons, then certainly this period of time in my life deserves the title. When I held Bess in my arms, naked or clothed, I felt assured that I was laying hold of a brilliant, a better, an unexpected world, never thinking that I was doing only what every other man had done and what had finally satisfied nobody.   (p. 128)

What could have been expressed with full cynicism is tilted towards the mood of the 'ordinary swoon', and an acceptance of how much and how little it can give. At the time, though, he demanded of Bess a world both 'certain' (p. 108) and 'unexpected', the resolution of complexity into delight which the landscape of the aerodrome seemed to have and which his village existence so failed to achieve. He is determined to maintain the idyll he has constructed around her, despite the continuing upheavals elsewhere. The scene in which the dying Squire sinks his teeth into his sister's hand, and is viciously beaten by her, convinces Roy of the final collapse of the old serenities:

> One action had revealed what I could never have suspected, a deep hatred for the man to whom she had, to all appearances, sacrificed her life ... What I had thought to be solid, rounded, and entire, now seemed to melt into frightful shapes of mist, to dissolve into intricacies wherein I was lost as though I had never been. At this intricacy I felt no wonder, but only bewilderment; and so I looked indifferently at the Squire's sister and at her brother's body. (pp. 123–4)

Such people cannot sustain the certainty he requires from them; they are not pure evergreens, but all sticky and peeling, and they cling to him unconscionably:

> 'How could I have done it?' she asked. 'How could I?' She spoke as though I were likely to know the answer to her question.
> 'One gets overwrought,' I said, conscious of the feebleness of my reply and irritated with her for requiring from me assurance in such a situation. (p. 124)

Roy's nerve of outrage is by now so dulled into mere indifference that he is no longer interested in tracing the truths behind these occasions, only in exerting his will to get clear of them. Even the news that Bess may be his sister provokes, after an initial shock, a determination to ignore it, a resolve simply to 'surmount this obstacle to my independence and my delight' (p. 157). 'Surmount' introduces a hint of flying over; as Roy listens to the revelation of his alleged incest, his eyes, in search of an object that will relieve some of the intensity of the moment and fix the scene by association for the future, settles on a bedcover: 'I began to pull at the loose threads on the patchwork quilt. The squares were red and yellow and blue' (p. 154) – gently proleptic of what he will shortly see of the village and its fields from the air, with the last loose threads cleared away.

His discovery of Bess's infidelity suggests to him, not that his demand for independence and delight was unattainable, but that she herself was in reality the greatest obstacle to it. For all his fleeting recognitions he had hardened himself to overlook those aspects of her life beyond the image he needed to make of her. The Flight-Lieutenant, now revealed not as the disengaged abetter of his love but a long-standing rival for it, has also forfeited much of his mystique by descending to Roy's level:

> Had the mass of ill-defined feeling which now overwhelmed me been, by some accident, concentrated into anger, I might well have killed him; as it was I thought of no such thing, but was puzzled as I looked at him, for previously I had admired his beauty, his experience, and his skill; I had looked up at him as at a superior being; but now I saw nothing superior in him, and was somewhat shocked to find it so.   (p. 163)

Between them, however, Bess and the Flight-Lieutenant have not destroyed the illusion of the superior being which Roy desires, but betrayed it, as his elders had done, reducing further the range of gilts he can invest in. Warner deftly inserts, among the familiar village noises Roy hears as he broods on this discovery, the sound of a whistle from the schoolroom which the Air Force has converted into a gymnasium; it acts as a kind of calling to attention of the distracted mind, a neat reminder of the nature and extent of the revolution in his old world that has occurred almost at the edges of vision, while Roy remained preoccupied with personal crises. He is still able to weigh up with his usual coolness the reasons for Bess's preference; the key is his rival's indifference, since 'while I had been only too anxious to reveal my feelings and declare my devotion, he by exercising restraint had increased his own value' (p. 170). For Bess, the aerodrome's indifference, its refusal of 'extravagant praise of those who are already sufficiently well-known', he has an attraction quite different from that of Roy's gauche romantic excesses; it offers her the chance of pleasure undeterred by moral and emotional complications. Not only is her view in this respect similar to Roy's, but the course of her career in the novel runs parallel to his own. She too gives up her village relationships in favour of something she imagines to be better, only to be disappointed and further entangled in the revelations of her birth and identity. But Roy, thinking only of what he calls her weakness and cruelty, cannot see the connection; he regards his own case as solitary and pure, aloof at last from untrustworthy attachments. He plunges into the river for a baptism, a cleansing of the stained body and a polishing of the new attitudes:

> I remember swimming under the water and groping along the bottom with my fingers at the mud and the roots of weeds with a strange feeling of exhilaration, and on the surface lying on my back, staring at the moon and the long leaves between it and me.
>
> (p. 173)

This bathe is like a ritual acting-out in miniature of his symbolic progress: upwards with a new mastery from the mud and roots at the bottom to the surface and the sky beyond, a transition between elements that requires only one more step to be complete, and this an aeroplane engine will provide.

Once he has joined the Air Force Roy encounters a fuller and more organised expression of attitudes and feelings that previously were suggested and hinted at. At first the recruits are made to experience seemingly pointless hardships, rather in the manner of the Foreign Legion; one toughens up and forgets the girl. But this is suddenly interrupted by a vision of glamour, no doubt highly potent among village boys of 1939 – an underground 'chapel', furnished like the most up-to-date cinema and brilliantly lit in Air Force colours, where the best cigarettes are provided free and waiters move quietly in the aisles, bringing without fuss whatever drinks are ordered. From this wholly secularised pulpit the Air Vice-Marshal dismisses the village associations – pulp, mud, sticky – in a manner that fully endorses the indifference to former attachments which Roy has sunk into, and makes of it a badge of new belonging and rank:

> "Reflect, please, that 'parenthood', 'ownership', 'locality' are the words of those who stick in the mud of the past to form the fresh deposit of the future. And so is 'marriage'. Those words are without wings. I do not care to hear an airman use them."
>
> (p. 178)

The Air Vice-Marshal encourages self-absorption as a joyous liberation from the choking grip of history, just as Roy had hoped during his first days with Bess, when everything outside him 'receded'.

Most of the Air Vice-Marshal's speech deals with sexual relationships; his man-of-the-world frankness is clearly designed to flatter
his young charges, and he favourably contrasts the self-control and
licensed hypocrisy of man with the passionate and servile nature of
woman: '"indeed, the construction of her body must inevitably
make her much more of a prisoner of time than you are
yourselves"' (p. 183). This gives Roy exactly the light he wishes to
see his relationship with Bess by. He can feel himself to have been
mildly rebuked for behaving immaturely with her, while congratu-
lating himself on having accurately assessed the Flight-
Lieutenant's more successful performance. Things fall into place
for Roy, as if he has found his vocation. He might be speaking not
only of his skills as a pilot, but of all the personal qualities most
admired at the aerodrome, of youthful iconoclasm and ruthless
disdain, when he declares 'I personally was at the right age and
had the right habits of nerve to be rather exceptionally proficient'
(p. 190).

He quickly utilises these new-found powers to revenge himself
upon the Flight-Lieutenant, starting an affair with his rival's new
love Eustasia wholly in the spirit of the Air Vice-Marshal's decree.
The previously only imagined promise of the aerodrome here
seems triumphantly fulfilled, as sex with Eustasia is both an
improved version of what he knows, and retains sufficient mystery
to startle and delight him:

> I was surprised and almost shocked to find the reality so much
> exceed the imagination in strength, in warmth, in vividness, and
> in surety of outline.   (p. 213)

The last phrase recalls the hangars set enticingly amid the uneven
hills; this at last is the new and clearer Nature, unfussy, rational,
and obedient to its own laws, which his long novitiate has secured
for him. In the sky there are no impediments to the perfect
regularity of line, nor murkiness and uncertainty of view. When
the Flight-Lieutenant begins to raise doubts about the aerodrome,
Roy now has the means to condemn out of hand the kind of
vacillation that had so long hampered him:

> We had reached the top of the hill, and I followed his gaze over
> the whole valley with the straight stripped alders marking the
> river channel as though for navigation, the dark woods and

curving pastures beyond. A heron rose flapping from the river. It was a midwinter windless day. I thought suddenly of how this valley would appear to me from the air and, looking at it again, felt a kind of distaste for its proximity, for its mud and reeds and the stifling nature of its life. A squadron of heavy bombers was coming towards us high overhead. I looked up at them, and heard the Flight-Lieutenant say in a somewhat apologetic tone of voice: 'I sometimes wonder what it's all for.'

    I kept my eyes on the bombers and smiled, as though he had spoken foolishly. (pp. 202–3)

Even before he 'suddenly' catches himself up into awareness of it, Roy cannot help noticing the features of the scene that remind him of flying; the language of the bomber squadrons was waiting for him to adopt it. There is something striking and disturbing about the ease with which his tone and vocabulary shift gear as his position in the Air Force becomes more secure and prominent – disturbing, because the abstract and carefully-balanced phrases he now uses to distance himself from humane involvement, and prepare the ground for possible evil, are only a slight refinement of his former habits and instincts, his persistent and fastidious drawing-back from commonplace or too-simply attainable pleasures. This freezing-over of his youthful puritanism is in its way more sinister than any of the Air Vice-Marshal's practised rhetoric. Roy reflects for example on how the Flight-Lieutenant, now working as the village padre,

spoke much of the villagers . . . often commending individuals for the most unlikely qualities, for fidelity that had no rational grounds, for an honesty that was merely the result of habit, for an uncritical acceptance of conditions that were merely imposed from above. I would often laugh at him, and indeed he found it difficult to defend his new tastes in any coherent manner . . . the familiar sight of the ground no longer moved me, for I felt the view restricted, remembering how clean, how remote, and how defenceless this country would seem from a great height in the air. (pp. 203–4)

When discussing with his leader the irritating recalcitrance of the Rector's wife and the Squire's sister, which the Flight-Lieutenant seemingly encourages, Roy talks of the possible 'transportation of the two ladies', and of the Flight-Lieutenant's having 'made remarks that might be construed in a sense prejudicial to our organisation' (p. 228). He is almost fully committed to a language designed to camouflage, like the hangars, its hidden intentions. More problematic still is the tone of his reflections on the murder, by the Air Vice-Marshal, of the Squire's sister. In this case Roy seems genuinely to believe that he is trying to think more deeply about it than his colleagues. The fact of the murder itself however leaves him quite cold; he regards it merely as an unpleasant act necessary to quell subversive behaviour. What instead 'still strangely moved me' is the thought of his having been present when it was committed. The whole sequence is a curious display of callous egotism posing as disinterested surmise:

> I was almost superstitious enough to imagine some fatality that seemed to bind me to these characters from my past, so that I had not been able to avoid being actually present at scene after scene of violence and stress in which they had been the chief actors.   (p. 238)

Roy never completely loses the reader's sympathy even in his deepest blindnesses, when he is overtaken by his concern to behave and think according to his leader's example. Just before these exchanges, the hitherto unchallenged belief in the superiority of the pilot and the esteem due to him was totally undermined by a demonstration of remote-controlled flying. This was the first indication that the airmen have not achieved freedom through mastery of self and the elements, but have enslaved themselves to a system whose technology has advanced so far that it is on the point of being able to reproduce itself, and will shortly have no further need of the skills and the attitudes the recruits have brought to it. (It gives among other things an ominous twist to the Air Vice-Marshal's insistence that 'no airman is to be the father of a child' (p. 181), which at first had seemed merely a liberating convenience.) So while Roy picks up the accents of importance, and dismisses his 'vague and irresponsible boyhood, full of pain but without direction or significance' (p. 240), his new status is already that of a dispensable cog in a vast machine whose own direction and significance remain obscure. This condition does at least assign the individual a temporary place, in which he can feel himself made greater by his sense of the forces working through and around him; but the benefits which he gains through the exertion of his will can only be maintained by submission to a more powerful will than his own. So when Roy is finally given a glimpse of 'what it's all for', it is the unprecedented grandeur of the idea that attracts him, the scale whereby particular and encumbering details are dwarfed and made trivial by the processes of an abstract power. This power, like the libocedrus, seems graciously to permit the worshipper to incorporate himself in its purity:

'We shall destroy what we cannot change.'

And as I listened to him I would feel that I understood more clearly now than before, when I was in the chapel, what it was at which we aimed. I remembered how from the air the valleys, hills, and rivers gained a certain distinction but wholly lost that quality which is perceived by a countryman whose day's travel is bounded by the earth of three or four meadows, and whose view for most of his life may be constricted by some local rising of the ground. In the air there is no feeling or smell of earth, and I have often observed that the backyards of houses or the smoke curling up through cottage chimneys, although at times they seem to have a certain pathos, do as a rule, when one is several thousand feet above them, appear both defenceless and ridiculous, as though infinite trouble had been taken to secure a result that has little or no significance.

I began to think now in the same way of those inhabitants of the earth who had never risen above it, never submitted themselves to a discipline like ours ... both their misery and their happiness seemed to me at this time in my life abject and pointless. (pp. 223–4)

This is the highest flight on which Roy embarks, and within it are signs anticipating his descent. He talks of the 'quality' of a countryman's perceptions, with a stirring of nostalgia for that proximity he tries to disparage. It recalls his earlier description of the Rectory garden, with its shabby-genteel earthiness, that had established his ambivalent attitude to what was too familiar; it was exactly that countryman's lack of curiosity as to what lies beyond or beneath his customary experience which Roy lost for ever when the Rector exploded the first bomb. There is still that ambivalence in the bold adventurers' yearning for some new, unknown region; still the pastoral rhythms of advancement and regression, as, disdaining 'the limits of their little reign ... still as they run they look behind'. The Flight-Lieutenant, no longer the brash and arrogant airman he once appeared, but now established as the spokesman for growing village dissatisfactions, takes up this idea in his sermons; the rising and falling curves of his and Roy's progress in the novel seem neatly to cross and overlap, like the gentle undulation of the hills all round them.

> 'So far as we can discover, this joy and this peace have actually been experienced by people living on the earth. How is it that we do not experience them? What is it that we have lost? These are questions that I must ask, but which I cannot answer' ... Here the Flight-Lieutenant paused and licked his lips ... it was evident that, in this mood, he could be of no use to us whatever.
>
> (pp. 231–2)

But Roy's present mood shares the same origin: 'Oh, I could have cried for joy and peace!' (p. 13). We do not pause to ask, on the first page of the novel, whether he cries for the having these things or the lack of them; his outburst seemed to lie so comfortably 'on the earth', with the smell, the mud, the reeds, the drunkenness. But the guardedness about letting go, which immediately followed it, is recalled by his harshness here towards what he regards as aimless and irresolute behaviour; even at the moments when he himself is least aware of it, the Roy of the aerodrome is recognisably the same person he always was.

Eustasia appeared to offer 'joy and peace', in the most immediately satisfying of the aerodrome's pleasures – sensual delight unrestrained by responsibility or distraction. When she becomes pregnant, in defiance of the Air Vice-Marshal's strictest edict, disturbances that had been evicted like the old man at the funeral force their way back in. Roy describes the effect in the now familiar terms, of something regular becoming uneven, or a smooth surface cracked:

> We were both of us aware that something new had come into our relationship, throwing suddenly out of all proportion what had previously appeared so symmetrical; or else that in a moment there had become apparent some flaw, hitherto unnoticed, and yet of so serious a kind as to reduce almost to nothing the value of something which had seemed precious.   (p. 252)

Roy's language here sustains two alternate, or simultaneous, possibilities: the flaw in the symmetry could tarnish something valuable, or it could rescue consciousness from a dangerous delusion. This ambivalence accompanies his rediscovery, from this point in his progress, of just the uncertainties, the mixed and conflicting feelings about the things he encounters, that he believed his commitment to the aerodrome had overcome. But all along that dual response to flaws and symmetries had remained embedded in the habits of perception which inform his narrative. When, for example, Roy met the Flight-Lieutenant at Eustasia's, he 'particularly noticed . . . that a white thread was clinging to the elbow of his uniform' (p. 212). While this acts as a kind of metonymic reminder of how the Flight-Lieutenant has disgraced his dignity as an airman by rubbing himself abjectly against a woman's clothing, it is also typical of the kind of thing Roy consistently notices – discrepant or incongruous details which stand out from or disturb the smoothness behind them. The 'loose threads' on the quilt earlier; the whistle among the familiar barking; Dr Faulkner 'rubbing the sleeve of his uniform against his ear' (p. 296), as he, Roy, and the Rector's wife wait in otherwise resolute silence for their likely execution; the Rector's wife listening to her husband's confession in a hiding-place where Roy 'could see nothing of her but three gleaming fingernails on which the light flickered' (p. 32); the hare on the grass (a telling reminiscence of the early-1930s hero Birkin: 'Don't you find it a beautiful clean thought, a world empty of people, just uninterrupted grass, and a hare sitting up?')[8]; the coconuts Roy struggles to conceal – various kinds of protuberance, by means of which the 'surveyor' reconstructs a moment in the memory, and which draw attention to symmetry or cleanliness by breaking or blemishing them. (It is perhaps worth mentioning here that the Rector's confession revealed how a similar kind of detail, with similar implication, had lodged in his mind for over 20 years; the man he was about to murder 'had a crumb at the corner of his mouth' (p. 35).) In the case of Eustasia's pregnancy, this 'flaw' will ultimately lead to Roy's escape from the aerodrome whose perfection it so offends, and thus prove a saviour rather than an obstacle. But the persistence in the writing of that intermittent anxious precision suggests that his hankering after the smooth and the orderly is never fully overcome; not even by his return to a suitably chastened Bess, with whom he finds a position of at least temporary balance between his

revulsion from imperfect things and the love they equally inspire
in him.

Although complications regather in his life, his manner of
expressing them only in part returns to the mingled puzzlements
and self-questionings of his pre-aerodrome days. He draws attention, for once, to the gap between his feelings at the time and his
account of them now; he appears slightly defensive about this,
unwilling to admit perhaps to the abiding influence of the Air Vice-
Marshal evident in the newly-confident rhetoric that is spread over
the obscurities:

> We in the Air Force had escaped from but not solved the mystery
> . . . we had banished inefficiency, hypocrisy, and the fortunes of
> the irresolute or the remorseful mind; but we had destroyed also
> the spirit of adventure, inquiry, the sweet and terrifying sym-
> pathy of love that can acknowledge mystery, danger, and
> dependence.
>
> So I thought as I gazed over the valley while waiting for the
> doctor, yet perhaps not so distinctly as I have set it down here.

The abstract language he now uses is a legacy of having been an
airman. It no longer indicates the icing-up of a mind that has lost
all meaningful contact with its surroundings, but it marks a further
stage in the search for a better distance from which to view them.
This gaze over the valley is one of several which punctuate the
book to assist measurement of Roy's progress; it proceeds now
from a midway point, neither too close to the ground, as when he
stumbled over the wire, nor too far away, as when he saw nothing
from the sky that did not look pointless and ridiculous. Roy has
travelled on an almost Wordsworthian journey, and ends it on the
gently raised eminence of the classical prospect poem, from which
vantage it appears that a regulated balance can be sustained,
between reason and nature, assertion and dependence, confidence
and uncertainty, air and earth:

> I, too, had regained what I had lost, a desire to see the world as it
> was and some assurance of the ground on which my feet were
> treading. It was not for me, I knew now, to attempt either to
> reshape or to avoid what was too vast even to be imagined as
> enfolding me, nor could I reject as negligible the least event in
> the whole current of past time . . . I remember that night as we

looked over the valley in the rapidly increasing darkness that we were uncertain of where we would be or what we would be doing in the years in front of us.   (pp. 301–2)

The smooth sentences which articulate this 'assurance', this way of seeing more 'distinctly', exude a kind of optimistic settlement. They gesture towards something they no longer wish to formulate or master absolutely, lest the effort to do so were to 'reshape' or distort what by its nature is complex and constantly changing. Yet there is still instability beneath. The 'rapidly increasing darkness', which might suggest the comfort of a familiar twilight suited to quiet meditation, cannot avoid indicating also the ominous closing-in of the 'years in front of us' from the autumn of 1939, in which this apparently successful circumventing of the totalitarian threat may seem only a minor skirmish. Roy's vague consciousness of a vastness that dwarfs him may yet contain a trace of his still unfulfilled desire to surrender his will to a superior power, one which may, despite his somewhat coy disclaimer, be after all 'not uninterested' in him. And if there is a play of forces which he can no longer attempt to avoid, it may yet take him in a direction where the lessons gained from this experience may be of limited value.

None of these undercurrents derives from conscious hypocrisy, but Roy was quite wrong to claim, in his earlier reflections 'over the valley', that hypocrisy was one of the things the aerodrome had successfully abolished. Had he not been so readily beguiled, he might have noticed how the Air Vice-Marshal, in his speech in the 'chapel', dwelt with such obsessive persistence on the details of the feminine world he claimed to despise. The Air Vice-Marshal has had intimate relations with both the Rector's wife and the Squire's sister, neither of whom he deigns to acknowledge in public. He has had a son by each of them; one of these he maintains in a rank beyond his merits, and places in the pulpit he himself once wished to occupy, while he creates for the other a sinecure of immense privilege, in complete disregard of normal and disinterested proce-dures for military promotions. He owns to neither of his sons, and preaches a creed which denies their existence; yet for all his resolution and lack of sentiment he cannot bring himself to dispose of them when they disobey him, except by underhand means. It transpires that his entire career as the master of a free and perfect system rests upon a falsification and suppression of the truth about the past more thoroughgoing than any perpetrated by the Rector or the Squire. This is the flaw in the regularity to which the Air Vice-Marshal cannot admit; he could only defend his position with the argument Roy himself had tried to employ on the night of the Rector's first breaking the news about him: 'Is not the fiction that has been firmly believed as good as true?' Even then, Roy 'can only say that I did not find it so' (pp. 19–20). The Air Vice-Marshal is sufficiently well-aware of how impressionable his elder son Roy is, how regularly his commitments tend to waver, to exhort him again, relating the muddy story with the directness that seemed so admirable:

> 'What a record of confusion, deception, rankling hatred, low aims, indecision! One is stained by any contact with such people. Can you not see, and I am asking you for the last time, what I mean when I urge you to escape from all this, to escape from time and its bondage, to construct around you in your brief existence something that is guided by your own will, not forced upon you by past accidents, something of clarity, independence, and beauty?'   (p. 295)

But precisely because of the relentless haunting of the airmen by the earthbound, to whose domain the planes must inevitably return, the aerodrome has failed to deliver the promised independence:

> I contemplated as he bade me the long record of crime and deception into which I had been born and had lived, but saw in that no reason to change my mind. If there had been guilt at the village, there had been guilt also at the aerodrome, for the two worlds were not exclusive, and by denying one or the other the security that was gained was an illusion.   (p. 295)

The two worlds are indeed not exclusive; like the chestnuts and the libocedrus they are nourished by the same soil. Each reminds the other of its shortcomings and of its aspirations; and each, in various conceivable forms, will be recurrently available, as products of or reactions to the other, since each will be built upon a desire to escape or improve what in the other is stained and confused. The Air Vice-Marshal is really asking Roy to separate his love from his aversion, by placing himself in such relation to objects that they can only inspire one or the other. But simply because of who he is Roy more than anyone cannot have unequivocal attachments. It is not open to him to deny either world, since he is the product of the union of the two. His identity is a blending of the seemingly irreconcilable; he feels 'united and at variance with' both his parents (p. 301). The melodramatic revelation, so long delayed, of the truth about Roy's origins, shows that it was his destiny, as much as it is his achievement, to be the link that proves the interdependence of all these ostensibly contrary states, which now appear locked in so deep a symbiosis that, as the deconstructors might have it, there is no saying which is the host and which the parasite.

So far I have been retracing the development of Roy's position by way of the successive situations he encounters and by using for the most part the terms and images he chooses. He has presented an essentially empirical progress, accompanied by occasional surmises, some earnest, some humorous, about the symbolic nature of certain perceptions or events. This progress has been activated by his uncertainty and discomfort, his consequent desire for order and clarity, and his discovery that the forms in which the latter appear to be offered in fact fail to do justice to his aspirations. The introduction, in the closing pages of the novel, of the idea of a destiny, now brings back into play larger and more continuously organised allegorical figurations in the novel, which my commentary has deliberately overlooked hitherto in order to concentrate initially upon the experience as Roy found it. It has been clear throughout how frequently he appeared to say more than he intended; how in his anxiety to escape restraints he unwittingly enmeshed himself in patterns of language and imagery – of outlines, flaws, regularity, precision – which established connections he was not explicitly making. Now his sense that what had been done was largely a mix of serendipity and his own free achievement is called further into question by the long-delayed revelation of his true parentage: the news that his birth and identity were not just mysteries that alienated him from former beliefs, but the sources of a complex chain of determinations leading him to where he now is. All the mingled contraries distributed through the novel now appear as if marshalled by a supervening relationship, or tension, between what is free and open in the story and what is circumscribed or forced into place.

This condition is reminiscent of *The Wild Goose Chase*, but its consequences are rather different. The suggestion that George's career developed according to recurrent and predictable patterns certainly added to the problems surrounding the resolution of that novel. But it manifested itself rather as a clog or obstruction tugging at the otherwise vigorous forward movement, over large, sparsely-inhabited distances, which supplied the narrative with its energy and enabled George, for all the uncertainty of his future, more readily to disentangle himself from the threats of restriction. Roy's movements by contrast are on a vertical rather than a horizontal axis. The changes in both seer and seen occur in a confined space where things crowd together. None of them can be so finally disposed of as some of their counterparts on George's travels. Because he does not meet with anything to which he can respond unequivocally and then move past, Roy does not have the kind of brisk, sceptical traveller's detachment which had saved George from the delusions his brothers suffered, and marked him as one always open to revolutionary reconstruction. In Roy's case it is only available as a bemused stare or a wilful self-forgetting. He never really learns to read the signs of his allegorical encounters in the way George does; he remains for much of the time a passive receiver of impressions, only briefly experiencing the kind of commitment to a set of ideas that enabled George to make such clear decisions about the world he moved through. The allegorical method in *The Aerodrome* is used less to give 'vigour and vividness to a definite belief', to use the terms of Warner's essay, than to 'partially reveal aspects of reality which elude, from their very complexity, the ordinary methods' (*The Cult of Power*, p. 110). Certain questions, moreover, about the proximity and correspondence of apparently separate things, bear more heavily than before upon the political themes of the novel. For example, in *The Wild Goose Chase*, the terms 'village' and 'city' may have wider than normal significance, but there was never any question that the relationship between them was more problematic than that of victim and oppressor. In that novel, the interfusion of states tended to produce infected or perverted conditions, like hermaphroditism, which it was part of the political task to reclarify. An allegorical mode which explains, orders, and to a degree systematically controls what would be oppressive by virtue of its indeterminacy, readily consorts with *The Wild Goose Chase*'s polemical intentions. But in *The Aerodrome* indeterminacy has a saving grace; the political and moral contract Roy comes to accept with the world, the positive ambivalence and open-endedness, appears to reject what the design of the novel relies on: a system of interlocking and self-sufficient patterns and replications that seems absolute and leaves nothing to chance.

For the allegorical texture of the novel is rather remarkably intricate. There are weavings and traceries that cover the relationships between characters, between careers, between separate or successive scenes, between single scenes and the larger project. In elucidating them it is possible to find something almost thrilling in the sheer audacity and extent of the contrivance. The Rector is killed by a gun from the aerodrome, wielded by the Flight-Lieutenant, one of two hidden sons of the Rector's old rival. This rival, now the Air Vice-Marshal presiding over the Rector's burial, is the man the Rector believed himself to have killed and consigned to earth (on two occasions, in fact; once on the mountainside and once in the churchyard). It takes a third plummet from the air to the ground to secure the Air Vice-Marshal's demise; this time his aeroplane, the symbol of the perfection that rendered man redundant, has been tampered with by the Flight-Lieutenant, who is now disillusioned with that perfection. The plane no longer responds to the controls; and the man who had failed to reconcile the conflicting values of earth and air, who had sought instead to secure one by suppressing the other, now suffers the fate of Icarus. The Air Vice-Marshal's crash has a catastrophic neatness as a dénouement, and also completes the pattern begun by his first fall from a height and its consequences for his outlook. Roy, by his change of mind, and the Flight-Lieutenant, by his act of sabotage, become literally what, as his unacknowledged sons, they always symbolically were, the flaws which doom the Air Vice-Marshal's system. The triangular relationship between Roy, the Flight-Lieutenant and Bess, is a 'curious modification' of the triangle 20 years previously involving the Rector, the Air Vice-Marshal and the Rector's wife, and Roy's reaction to being betrayed – betrayed indeed on the night before his secret marriage – follows a similar course to his father's. (Roy at least has the chance to enlist in someone else's system rather than having to construct his own; in this novel it is the fathers who have the grand designs.) As for the Rector's wife and the Squire's sister – both of whom are known only in connection with the relationships they have been forced to accept, their names disguising their true desires – their mysteriously ambiguous behaviour towards the aerodrome is explained by the discovery of their past intimacies with the Air Vice-Marshal. I mentioned in passing how Bess's career resembled Roy's; she is also linked with the Air Vice-Marshal, as, having been betrayed in an apparently secure relationship, she falls into a semi-comatose state from which she is rescued by the ministrations of Dr Faulkner (this is one of the weaker and less convincing sections of the book, drawn out principally to let Dr Faulkner reappear). The Flight-Lieutenant, Roy's alter ego before he is revealed to be his half-brother, has perhaps the most fully-developed role in the allegory. He begins by representing the attractive power, independence and assurance of the aerodrome; he complicates that attraction by turning out to be a mediocre airman, showing off among the villagers to compensate for his lack of status elsewhere. He takes over the role of the Rector and denounces the aerodrome from the village pulpit; finally, after committing his sabotage, he attempts to escape from the constraints of his life, as the Rector before him had done, in the company of a woman who does not love him and who is pregnant by another man. And since the Air Vice-Marshal had actually been awarded the living in the first place, and was supplanted by his would-be murderer, it seems perfectly proper that the Rector should have been succeeded by the man who actually killed *him*, as part of a large and continuous pattern of people being worsted in their ambitions and desires by their real or symbolic rivals.

Successive scenes in the novel are similarly bound together in the allegory. A simple example is the Flight-Lieutenant's killing the Rector at the exact moment when Roy makes love with Bess for the first time; each of Roy's rites of passage is marked by an episode in the continuing struggle between aerodrome and village. There is a more involved case of this connection when, after hearing that Bess may be his sister, Roy decides not to seek confirmation of this report, but to remain instead in the kind of doubt that would give his life with Bess the elements of mystery and adventure he later more explicitly calls for. No sooner does he resolve to make positive use of his uncertainty, rather than reaching irritably after facts, than he discovers that the Flight-Lieutenant has been cuckolding him from the beginning. Once again the aerodrome intervenes at a crucial moment, simultaneously providing Roy with a means of escape, and destroying the value of what his escape was intended to enhance.

Such moments allow for unwitting intimations, in Roy's personal life, of what will subsequently surface as the general theme. The most substantial of the allegorical miniatures in which the larger scope of the novel is prefigured is the scene of the Rector's confession. Almost all the subjects which acquire later prominence are introduced here, many in a humorous or burlesque form. Roy only eavesdrops upon the confession because his shame at abandoning his birthday dinner led him to creep back into the Rectory through a study window; it shows aptly and comically enough how each step in his progress is predicated upon the previous one, and that his freedom of manoeuvre is limited not least by what James in *The Ambassadors*, capturing with similarly winning innocence the high comedy of his moment, called 'the accidents of a high civilisation . . . the frequent exposure to conditions . . . in which relief has to await its time'.[9] The Rector himself, in an ominous anticipation of Roy's later career, resembles, while speaking, 'some delicately adjusted machine now perfectly fulfilling the task for which it had been designed' (p. 28). He petitions God's aid in making him 'clean' from contradictory emotions, as he continues to think of his crime with as much fascination as loathing (and, Claudius-like, wishes still to enjoy its fruits). He is linked with Roy by way of the kind of precise detail he notices (the crumb on Anthony's mouth, the way he smoothed his hair), and through certain locutions which constantly pull his speech in the direction of air and flight. He wishes that his transgressions may be 'even . . . as a windless calm' (p. 30); Roy reaches the peak of his complacency watching bombers on 'a midwinter windless day' (p. 203). When discussing with Anthony the fulfillment of God's work on earth, the Rector 'spoke . . . with particular fervour of a certain reredos in which were depicted white doves ascending from and descending into a chalice of wine' (p. 35). Looking down from a great height upon similar villages and fields to those Roy will see, the Rector forgets God's 'mercy and enormous power', being 'deafened by my blood and by the roaring of my pride' (p. 35) into exasperation at the haplessness of those below him. Meanwhile, since the Rector is confessing to a murder he greatly desired but actually failed to commit, the whole of his account, systematically repeated every year, is flawed in a manner analogous to all the other systems in the novel, in being designed to express and put into clear order something that has not in fact been achieved.

A similar point could be made about the grocer's lament and the Air Vice-Marshal's proclamations. Such speeches do not function in quite the same way as the statements made about their motives and beliefs by allegorical characters in the earlier books. While those, humorous or serious, presented public arguments with which the hero could in various ways engage, in these 'confessions' the element of rhetorical construction or masking is more apparent, and the hero's encounter with them less direct. The speeches all represent in a sense summings-up or crystallisations of something which is properly obscure and muddy. Each is born from a mutual concern to submerge the confusions of personal experience in the consoling orders of ritual. All three speakers desire that they and the worlds they inhabit, large or small, should be 'clean'; they have all clearly so perfected their performances that they can be reproduced to order; all three, wilfully or through ignorance, find themselves divorced by these rituals from the experience that impelled them. The narratives they called up as servants come to take on a life of their own; and the allegory overall, which reveals the shortcomings in Roy's account, is itself the most relentlessly self-generating and multiplying of all these systems, refuelling in mid-air as it were, tracing out its perfect curves to its own contentment, while gazed on in bewildered fascination by the subject it no longer requires.

It was just that kind of remote control, that effortless avoidance of hazard, which caused the aerodrome itself to be seen as an escape from the mysteries on which it was founded, rather than the solution to them it promised to be. This is why I think the image of Roy staring incredulously up at a sky filled with pilotless planes has such enduring pathos and power, and why his final response to the aerodrome has to be a turning away in regret. Turning away, because it has failed to accommodate the man in his desires; regret, because a condition in which that problematic humanity no longer matters, in which there is balm for hurt minds, remains perennially alluring. What Roy now wishes to trust in is a love which accepts aversion as its necessary complement. This love can only survive so long as some aspect of its object remains unclear, as the object which is known and explained does not satisfy desire but produces indifference; it excludes the desire which is subsequently redirected elsewhere. The Air Vice-Marshal himself proposed that 'the knowledge of complete power is the beginning of the end of love' (p. 185), and when Roy returns to Bess he finds the possibility of love at the point where power and certainty disappear. The generations whose efforts had resulted in the 'fumbling conventions' (p. 261) of village life are seen as having been driven by the same ambitions for security as have produced the aerodrome. But each successive mode of establishing order amid the uncertainties can only last so long, before its sham perfection eases itself away from those who try to live with it. It either grows rigid and mechanical, or it breaks down under the pressure of inner disorders over which the sheet of purity has been thrown. There is a certain implicit optimism in Roy's reflections that this process may become almost classically Hegelian, but there can be no clear confidence about the progressive shape of the future; nor is the attitude any longer desired that would substitute such neat conventions for the fumbling ones.

And in like ways the allegorical structure of the novel remains in ambiguous relation to the views which emerge from it. Roy commends the virtues of the adventurous and the unexpected, while the writing pulls back towards discipline and order; the same allegory which undermines one aspect of the totalitarian dream – that the self could be liberated from the nets that entangle it – goes some way towards covertly endorsing another, that the self should find its true significance as a tiny, uniformed and submissive part of a vast system that can proceed regardless of the local fallibility of its components. Roy's account does not allow him to rest securely upon what he intended it to say; the craving for order and pattern continues, in tension with the rebelliousness which is simultaneously provoked. The hillside vantage Roy arrives at may compose them into harmonious balance, or may merely be the temporary settlement of an unstable mixture. The novel knows that what the aerodrome represents is still attractive, still part of a latent desire, and that only by accepting the attraction can an alternative be honestly fought for.

Notes

1. *The Letters of T. E. Lawrence*, ed. Garnett, London 1938, p. 853; this quotation from a letter to Robert Graves of 4 Feb. 1935.
2. Rex Warner was interviewed by Hugh Hebert in the *Guardian* of 2 November 1974.
3. Anthony Burgess, introduction to *The Aerodrome*, Oxford 1982, p. 12.
4. Angus Wilson, introduction to *The Aerodrome*, The Bodley Head, London 1966, p. 10.
5. Burgess, p. 9.
6. G. W. Stonier, 'The New Allegory', in *Focus One*, ed. Rajan and Pearse, London 1945, p. 29.
7. Virgil, Eclogue IV, line 13.
8. D. H. Lawrence, *Women In Love*, edition of Cambridge UP 1987, p. 127.
9. Henry James, *The Ambassadors*, Penguin 1986, p. 153.

5

War and its Aftermath –
Why Was I Killed? and
Men of Stones

In *The Aerodrome* the allegory was like an aeroplane; for good and ill
it lifted one to a view of the scene available nowhere else, and too
rarefied to be indefinitely combined with other human needs. At
the close of the book the long view was ostensibly abandoned in
favour of a cautious and reluctant assent to current conditions.
These provided at least a chance for meaning and purpose to
develop, even while they simultaneously placed obstacles in the
way, or nurtured aspirations whose full realisation might prove
incompatible with the circumstances that gave birth to them. Roy
could allow 'meaning' and 'purpose' to remain as unbreached
abstractions, towards which certain routes have failed to lead; he
lives now in a state of potential which grants him a temporarily
safe patch of ground from which to survey the alternatives. But in
Warner's next fictional work, *Why Was I Killed?* (1943), a similar
retrospective investigation of some of the avenues that have led to
the present state is conducted by one whose own potential has
been suddenly cut off. Roy's form of negative capability – his
openness and his leisure to wait – has now to meet some harder
questions. This book's narrator is the ghost of a soldier killed in the
Second World War. In his last moments he has had a vision of the
bright and dark sides of the life he is leaving, crystallised into
perfectly commonplace images: a summer valley on the one hand,
his own broken and blood-smeared body on the other. It is the
starkness of this contiguity, the apparent challenge to the significance of each image by the other, that impels him to put –
notionally at least – the question of the book's title to the members
of a party visiting a monument to the Unknown Soldier in an
English cathedral. The six members of this party comprise a kind of
miniature provisional 'democracy'; they represent various opinions and stations within it, often so different from one another as

112

to be almost completely opposed, yet bound together by the fact of the war and by the more or less realised sense of common purpose it gives them. The ghost of the soldier regards each of these civilians as morally responsible for the battles being fought on their behalf; he seeks from them a form of reassurance that his own life and death had a meaning which can be made articulate in their continuing existence. The book that results is in no conventional sense a novel. Warner subtitled it a 'dramatic dialogue', but the dialogue, or round-table debate, between the representative figures is really only the top crust. In the bulk of the work the soldier conducts a silent interrogation of each figure in turn, tracing through their past lives for the forces and combinations of experience that have led them to the views they hold. None of these fully convinces him, but the process of patient diagnosis itself has a certain power to console, if only by relieving him of some aspects of his isolation.

It is a curious book, and presents evident problems. It appeals to popular comprehension while making no concessions to popular taste; its uncertain category makes it difficult to assimilate to conditions other than those of its immediate occasion. But although it is often weighed down by an earnestness unrelieved by humour or spontaneous invention, there are still moments of unusual power and interest. The schematic construction, beginning with the device whereby the observer is artificially and irrevocably distanced from the activities he reflects upon, suggests something much more stagey and evasive than is actually found; the contrivance rarely intrudes upon the reading. There is nothing whimsical about the work, nor, excepting some lapses, does it exude the musty and faded drawing-room atmosphere that renders quite disinterrable so many of the once-fashionable symposium-plays it ostensibly resembles. If anything it is almost excessively austere and scrupulous in its refusal to take up any of the opportunities for fanciful entertainment or cheap effect that its project offers. It has the character of an act of mourning, a privately conducted yet ceremonial working-through of a grief which is generally shared; it is not afraid to take the risks – not all of which it surmounts – of its extreme bareness, and to tackle directly the simple and the obvious.

This places the text in the company of the essays Warner wrote during the war, the bulk of which were revised and collected in *The Cult of Power* (1946). They broke little new ground, but offered a

simplified digest of his principal literary and political concerns. The
war seemed to provoke in Warner a newly self-conscious and sober
sense of responsibility to maintain what he could of the purpose-
fulness that had motivated the literature of ideas in the previous
decade, and to resound the call for the writer to occupy a place at
the centre of affairs, precisely at the time when he or she was most
likely to be regarded as a distraction or even as seditiously critical.
Literature had become for him an essential public service which, in
the post-war reconstruction, ought to be subsidised by the State, as
it should never, for its own survival, have to abandon its 'political
task . . . to show men how they live and what is meant by their own
words and manners' (*The Cult of Power*, p. 129). But in all these
writings the optimistic determination of 'never again' is subdued
by the ironic echo of 1919 and the League of Nations, and by
Warner's increasingly explicit uncertainty about the merits of any
political programme; in the most substantial essay, 'Dostoyevsky
and the Collapse of Liberalism', he rehearses in discursive form
some of the propositions that had appeared in his earlier novels,
with even less confidence that the gap left by the decline of religion
could be adequately filled.

Why Was I Killed? shares in this implicit turn towards the pulpit,
the source of Warner's earliest exposure to the patient disciplines
and the rhythmic beguilements of rhetorical argument. The writing
seems to proceed from a state of suspension, a place set apart; its
stylised remoteness is deliberately heightened. The characters are
more purely illustrative of typified positions than in any of the
other works, partly because the narrator can have no active contact
with them and can see them only across an unbridgeable distance.
The only moment in which they collide is the moment of his
question, put to the living on the soldier's behalf by a priest
granted conventional intercessionary powers; it is the question
itself which concentrates and reduces the characters, so that what
is shown of them is only what essentially enables them to answer
as they do. There is no claim that the whole identity of these
characters has been exposed; rather that the degree to which they
might incorporate more than is revealed here, or might merge and
overlap with each other instead of remaining, as they do, starkly
separate, is not pursued. It is only in the soldier's mind that any
such complication or interweaving occurs, in a constant tension
with his anxiety to disentangle the knot into its basic component
threads – an anxiety which the book strangely convincingly

suggests might well be true of a disembodied spirit struggling for peace.

The problem that haunts the other novels, of where the vantage-point can be found from which the desired survey might be possible, is simply shelved by the device here of wrenching the overlooking consciousness out of the world altogether. The height from which it sees is no longer complicit with the structures of power it is analysing, nor with a voluntary, Lucretian detachment, from which categories are imposed or distinctions blurred. Unlike for example Frankenstein or Gregor Samsa, two more spectacular frustrated aliens, this soldier has neither the capacity nor, for the most part, the desire to intervene in the world on which he comments. The narrative is punctuated by odd moments – quite eerie for being so matter-of-factly mentioned – when the characters seem vaguely aware of his presence among them, as if within each critical turn or swerve in the development and hardening of their views were a flicker of consciousness of the dead to whom they are responsible. The ready access to the surfaces of their lives which the narrative convention affords him is at these moments cut across by a glimpse of pathos; each world searching for comfort from the other which neither can find. He is only tentatively calling those below him for judgement; it is the difficulty of his question which preoccupies him as much as the quality of the replies. His long view largely resembles that of an archaeologist, patiently excavating and absorbing layers of evidence about people who seem only intermittently familiar, and who appear to be 'drifting and shuffling, rather as corks or sticks upon a slow current than as if with deliberate intent' (p. 16) – as if it was they, not he, who were dead, and the substance and meaning of their lives had to be painstakingly reconstructed from the outside:

> He stopped speaking and, as he looked across the room at the others, his face expressed both sorrow and bewilderment. His friend was tapping the wood of his walking-stick with the fingers of his right hand, while with his left he made the stick gently rotate. There was a look of strain in his eyes and again he seemed at a loss for words. I thought that there was something terrible in the resignation of his posture and in the quiet voice which I had just heard. These men seemed to me like sentient things that know themselves ineluctably held and clasped in the workings of some vast regardless machine.   (pp. 97–8)

Edwin Muir, always an enthusiast for Warner's work, wrote of the 'curious light' cast by prose like this[1]; inessentials seem to be whitened-out, or fall into a shadow which sets off what is left. The blankly forensic recounting of appearances, the suggestion of an unreachable and already discounted emotion behind them, the minimal or numbed security afforded by the repetition of routine movements, all register a tacit sympathy across the gulf between observer and observed; the writing and the behaviour it reports seem equally painful and necessary responses to an external compulsion before which they are alike helpless. The cumulative effect of this patient bareness can stimulate quite comple responses for the reader who feels the weight of compassion the writing is concerned to restrain rather than indulge. In the scene just before the above quotation:

> 'When I think of the last war,' she said, 'I cannot help thinking of an old woman whom I used to visit. Her son had been reported missing, and she could do nothing but sit indoors on her chair, rocking herself to and fro. "My boy," she'd say, "where is my boy?" and nothing we could say to her was any good. In the end she died. That kind of thing is very terrible.'
>
> She stopped speaking and looked down to the floor, pursing her lips together. It seemed that she had spoken almost involuntarily and now wished to recall her words. (p. 96)

– or, at the close of the story of the munitions worker and his wife, where the narrator watches the girl's realisation of how fettered and unfulfilled her life has become. No relief is offered her beyond submission to her husband's version of 'new realism'; while the soldier, in a flourish of purple, ironically draws attention to the idea that the dead, for all their unrestricted view, have even less access to an ultimate meaning than do the living:

> Bob Clark spoke authoritatively. 'Don't be soft,' he said. 'Don't think. Why should you? It doesn't pay. Thinking won't alter things. You've got a nice house, haven't you? We're not doing too badly, are we?'
>
> She shuddered slightly and looked up, past the furniture, to the ceiling of the room as though it were the roof of a trap . . . it seemed to me that her eyes were endeavouring to pierce through the plaster and woodwork that lay between them and the view

of the night. I could have told her what she would see if she could see as I did – a vast vault of blackness studded, in the incredibly remote distance, with the flickering light of gigantic and incalculably numerous worlds.   (pp. 90–1)

The ideas and arguments in *The Professor* were presented as a series of independent attacks, from different angles, on a single point; the structure thus generated mimed the crisis involved, where liberalism's willingness to entertain its opponents was rapidly converted into a crowding-out of the space in which it had imagined itself the host. In *Why Was I Killed?*, which in its character of 'novel of ideas' is closer to *The Professor* than to Warner's other works, the organisation rather resembles a slow deposition of strata in a landform. Each layer of attitude and proposal remains separate while affecting the structure of the whole; each has a certain influence on the shape of its successors, while simul-taneously modifying those on which it settles. The initial stages of this development contain much that is dull and monotonous. The book takes a long time to gather momentum, because the earlier subjects of the soldier's enquiry are the less interesting and sympathetic; Warner seems also to have lost much of his old relish for caricature in dealing with them. Hence the story of Fothey, the elderly captain of industry, falls rather flat. There are some routine vignettes of the First World War, and of the political complaints of Warner's generation against their elders (voiced here, unusually, by a woman). The narrator himself is less censorious, seeing 'both the confident geniality' of the opulent late-Victorian world 'and the instability of the bases on which it rested' (p. 40), but while Fothey's cast of mind is effectively typical, both in its prejudices and in its inability to see when a prejudice is being disconfirmed, he offers nothing for the reader to be curious about. He is just sensitive enough, when challenged, to admit some uneasiness about his role in the world, but he could never overcome his instinctive support for the status quo, a support bred into him and persisting in the face of experiences which might as easily have caused disillusionment. Meanwhile an officer disabled in the First World War, and struggling to reintegrate himself into a society of whose shortcomings he is doomed to be a constant reminder, shows the ghostly narrator a more explicit motive for the guardedness of his own discourse:

I knew the effort of will which lay behind his most ordinary

words, the restraint which he was setting always upon a mind
which, without that restraint, would, he thought, whirl away
into irresponsibility and inarticulateness.   (p. 46)

The anxious pedantry of the prose here acts out the condition it
describes.

Warner was not at his happiest when attempting to portray the
urban working class, and the story of Bob Clark, like that of
Fothey, sounds too many thin and inauthentic notes. It does,
however, produce a subtler portrait than might have been expected from a tale ostensibly illustrating the stunting of talent by
an unjust system. Clark's impoverished family persuade him to
abandon a promising school career for a steady job; he subsequently
comes to regard the learning he has given up, not with crude
contempt or envy, but simply as something he has no need for. His
decision has indeed resulted in exactly what his parents hoped for
him. Only his wife, in the petulant defiance with which she cheers
him on in front of the other cathedral visitors, betrays any
suppressed awareness of his selfish complacency, its origins and
its possible outcome. Clark's manners are of his time but his type
is not difficult to recognise. Nor is that of the European scholar's
son who is gradually indoctrinated with fascist ideals. The mixture
of ambition and frustration which drives the boy towards totalitarianism is familiar from the earlier books; so is the uncertainty that
returns when the exercise of will has been abrogated, as the
narrator comments: 'nor was there anything more admirable in the
qualities of indecision and insincerity because I had found examples of evil in their opposites' (p. 110). *Why Was I Killed?* only really
begins to raise its energies with the accounts of the Spanish Civil
War veteran and the pacifist widow.

The 'Man from Spain' is shown in two scenes – arguing for
revolutionary socialism with a university friend in the 1920s, and
writing further reflections on their debate 15 years later, after the
Republican defeat. The first episode might be, say, E. M. Forster
talking with Ralph Fox, but it has also the accents of a more
personal disenchantment; the older speaker presents the puzzled
liberal case as from one who has been through all the stages his
young friend is about to enter, rather as Warner and his friends in
1943 might have conversed with their own youth. The debate is
strongly articulated on both sides, and the uneasiness in the
relationship between the speakers, their struggles to restrain

impulses towards patronage and resentment, gives their conversation a genuine edge lacking in the book's earlier sections. The older man is unswayed by his companion's idealism, but has an acute sense that his own contribution, because it necessarily lacks finish and conviction, sounds uncomfortably like the complacency that regularly accompanies thwarted hope:

> when good men
> On every side fall off, we know not how,
> To selfishness, disguised in gentle names
> Of peace and quiet and domestic love,
> Yet mingled not unwillingly with sneers
> On visionary minds.

(*The Prelude*, II, 451–6)

In this case the liberal does not sneer, as he has too much pity for his friend. But as the younger man dimly suspects, the pity, while truly compassionate, is also an instrument for keeping its object down to a safe level, whereby the pitier's own insecurity and lack of achievement can be naturalised and made to seem just and inevitable (to switch rather abruptly from Wordsworth to Blake, 'pity would be no more/if we did not make somebody poor'). As usual with Warner's protagonists, they are implicated in the struggles of more forces than their rhetoric encloses; the soldier who listens is mildly surprised by his own even-handedness, as after so much disappointment he has at last found attitudes to life which quicken his sympathies. 'How rarely it was, I reflected, that people failed to speak the truth, and how strangely at variance, each from each, were the truths which they expressed!' (p. 119). Amid conditions of war which stimulate the search for an image of stability which is not stasis, which is released from the vicissitudes of political enforcement, Warner alludes frequently to Heraclitus, with his leaps across the middle ground, from local illustration to universal pattern: 'They do not apprehend', claims fragment 51, 'how being at variance it agrees with itself; there is a connection working in both directions, as in the bow and lyre'.[2] (This also recalls Roy's concluding sense of being 'united and at variance with' both his parents.) The socialist, writing his letter after 15 years, refuses to allow the defeat of his cause (in the Spanish Civil War) to stand as proof of its futility. On the contrary, the experiences conventionally 'sobering' have in many ways strengthened his original beliefs. He accurately predicts how the significance of his movement will be rapidly denigrated and trivialised by those whose interests are served by mocking the supposed naivety of others. Warner succeeds here in creating a mood of conviction whereby his character seems to have earned the right to say things that otherwise might sound platitudinous and vapid. In the coming war,

> splendid ideals will be set before (men) to encourage them to fight the more resolutely. I am inclined, as I said, to doubt whether what might most help them will be put before them, the story of our army, who fought from their own hearts on foreign soil, hoping for the possibility of peace and believing in the dignity of man. Yet our army existed and that is what matters.
>
> (p. 128)

The narrator is impressed but not won over; his own experience as a soldier was far from the coherence and single-mindedness of socialism, containing as it did elements that would sit uncomfortably within the 'vision of ordered justice' which the veteran kept before him. The narrator discovered what the fascists exploited – as in Vander's speech in *The Professor* – that humanitarian aims alone were not sufficient to inspire allegiance; he sees also the crusting-over of the heart in the veteran's too-long sacrifice, the turn away from the 'colour, intricacy and delight' (p. 131) of his own perception of life. The inflexibility of the grand idea still incites respect, even admiration, but no longer the desire to follow it or to hand personal anxieties into its care; it is attacked by the pacifist widow for its cruelty and hypocrisy after scarcely pause enough for its cadences to register.

This woman, who has lost both husband and son in successive wars, presents a case that rests less on intellectual conviction, prejudice, or even plain emotionalism, than on a dogged concern, struggling to find an adequate form of words, to resist the abstracting tendency altogether and to hold on simply to what can be securely known. Of all those present she is the one most reluctant to take part in the debate at all, and most aware of the ease with which her feelings can be made to seem trite and flimsy when brought to the surface for inspection. She began by saying 'I think sometimes that we do not want to live, and that it will take more than politics to cure this' (p.33); she is uncertain whether it is 'something in nature', or, as she later begins to suspect, the whole construction of society and culture which leads men to dissipate their most admirable qualities in destructiveness, to turn their backs on life and 'die for some kind of an idea which they themselves do not understand' (p. 33). There are signs that Warner here, without moving much beyond the conventional image of the woman as a protective mother, more concerned with her immediate sphere of interest than with wider questions, is putting out feelers towards a feminist argument – the kind presented in more recent times and in more rigorously analytical form in Christa Wolf's *Cassandra*, for example. Here one of the principal causes of war, and thus answers to the soldier's question, is the historically-engendered expectations men have of themselves, and the speed with which these can be crystallised into ideal images and objects of worship by a patriarchal society which is anxious to propagate its exclusive vision by naturalising its own distortions and pre-empting the right to comment. In such conditions the alternative, female voice has no chance to be heard. It is driven either from the arena or from the language or 'serious' debate; its questioning of male assumptions is either not listened to or not regarded as a question.

The development of the woman's story certainly gives rise to such reflections. Warner traces movingly and with care her increasing bemusement at the mixture of desperation and resignation her sufferings produce in her. At first she has a confidence deriving not only from her love but from her capacity, unlike Bob Clark's wife, to defeat her husband in argument, both on his terms and hers. As they question whether or not he should join up in 1914, we are shown the assumptions of superiority that underlie her husband's tenderness towards her, how real their mutual affection is and how routinely he exploits and blackmails with it, the evasive bluster with which he responds to remarks of hers that puncture his ego with uncomfortable illuminations:

'Men will behave like wild beasts when they are maddened by fear and unreality. On both sides it will be the same thing. Haven't you got to behave like a wild beast when you charge with a bayonet?'

He did not answer this question. Instead he spoke with a note of anger in his voice. 'You're all mixed up,' he said. 'You're arguing as though I was maintaining that war is a good thing.'

(p. 143)

Her confidence is burnt out by her failure to influence her husband at a time when there is still a choice as to whether to become involved in war or not – unlike the soldier's own case, as he with slight asperity points out. Her desperation is twisted further by the muted sense that her husband's decision was affected by the very eloquence of her appeal, her rhetorical powers themselves regarded as a threat to his manhood. And in the later case of her son, those powers have dwindled into a tentative anxiety; her pacifist convictions struggle for articulacy in the face of moral points in favour of fighting whose worth she knows she must concede. She can no longer hope for a secure enclave for herself, nor offer her son anything more positive than war and violence to overcome the aimless drifting which has characterised his peacetime life. Her story is much the most painful of those the soldier examines; not only on account of her sufferings, but because she alone of the disputants finds the source of her values in the experiences least amenable to discussion, and is isolated by the lack of a secure language for precisely the things she most wishes to communicate:

> I say I cannot bear to read the papers nowadays, and yet I often do read them. But how I hate their cruel headlines and their smug articles, all the big words which are day by day persuading people that war is not a crime. They are like fetters on people's minds and people are so loaded with them that they cannot move towards the good and simple things which the heart sees. Instead they drag themselves clumsily among the big words and forget their own hearts.   (p. 165)

The writing here is not afraid to risk the sentimentality, by which we would regard its naive pathos as something tame and exploited, for the sake of its truer appeal which cannot frame itself in any other form.

In *Why Was I Killed?* women's voices are heard at greater length, if not across a much greater range, than in Warner's previous novels. Women as love-objects are throughout viewed essentially sentimentally, as in much of the fiction of the period. Their roles divide between earthy English rose, called something solid like Joan or Bess, and exotic foreign temptress, with a name ending in 'a' – Marqueta, Clara, Eustasia. Although there is no real deviation from the stereotype, there are occasional stirrings within it. Marqueta, for instance, in *The Wild Goose Chase*, is only half-committed to the part she is cast in, and plays it for much of the time in a state of hypnotic compulsion; elsewhere she reveals a capacity for thought and argument at odds with the air of helplessness about her behaviour. The glimpse of a conflict in her of aspiration and entrapment contributes to the sense of wasted potential which only revolution, it is there believed, can remedy. Eustasia likewise casts some lingering glances at Bess, suggesting not merely that she really wanted to be Roy's contented wife all along and that this is the only female destiny worth having, but that for her as much as for Roy and the Flight-Lieutenant the aerodrome has created another form of slavery under the guise of freedom. Bess herself is a pale character, rather evasively treated in the latter part of the novel in order that Roy's progress should continue without further hindrance. But she is allowed a slightly more complex experience than he imagines her to have. She suffers her own independent frustrations with her allotted place and expectations, feelings accompanied but not wholly disposed of by the account of her Perdita-like disguised origins. These frustrations promote in her also ambivalent responses; there is indeed a muted but chastening note in the novel, as Roy dimly realises that Bess looks upon *him* as symptomatic of all that is clinging and suffocating about village life. But the changes they go through are not permitted to part them; one feels, as with a number of his characteristics, that Roy's resistance to the idea of Bess's fuller individuality is shared by his creator. Warner is rather more convincing in his presentation of the older women in *The Aerodrome*. The Rector's wife and the Squire's sister, although tightly bound to their allegorical roles, display a moral authority in the face of their dilemmas which challenges Roy's more fragile and narcissistic reactions, and which is as much enhanced as diminished by the comic treatment they are occasionally subjected to. Their mixed response to the Air Vice-Marshal is quite unlike Roy's restless fascination. The experience of love allows them to combine a firm loyalty to the man with an implacable opposition to everything he does and stands for; it requires more strength of character than Roy ever possesses. The passing revelations of its cost to them appear to Roy rather as annoying disturbances of the tranquillity he requires to cultivate his own projects, than as breakings to the surface of desires and frustrations deeper than his own, which the women's integrity, as much as their parochial routine, has held in check. These two women and the widow of *Why Was I Killed?* give glimpses of a reservoir of sympathy Warner leaves largely untapped, partly because the stunting or perversion of such feeling, either by choice or by external intervention, is a continuous undertow in his writings.

The soldier rejects the pacifist argument; like the widow's own son he knows that he cannot opt out of the demands of his time. But he does regard her, though in some ways the most divided from him in opinion, as the closest in sensibility. The end of his exploring seems to have been to arrive where he started, but without the security of firmer understanding; he finds himself both moved by and implicated in the woman's predicament, that

> the world which she saw as beautiful and forgiving had taken forcibly from her just the things which she most valued, and left her no substance, only the memory of certain moments and of an incomplete devotion.   (p. 173)

The priest, who by convention is able to talk directly to the soldier, offers some reassurance towards knowing the place for the first time; his sympathetic insight allows the soldier to recognise that the initial vision of light and dark, which he had felt to be solitary and problematic, is potentially available to all, and could provide a focus for human contact rather than an enforced isolation: 'My picture was no longer one that might be painted by a contemplative or an aesthete or by the imagination of regret. It was a world which would be created or discovered as it was either suddenly or gradually perceived' (p. 191). But as a conclusion it seems hurried and obscure, expressing rhetorical relief rather than anything more substantial; it knows the problems raised through the book are not bought off by it. Religion underpins the priest's view of companionship and its meaning, but his ordinary humanity is what enables him to share the soldier's vision; when they part the soldier turns away from the altar towards the human world. Warner's respect for Christian faith, recovered through the war years, is unwavering, but not until the last line of his last novel, *The Converts* (1967), does he declare unequivocally for it. The only effective answer which this soldier's question can receive is that Heraclitean sense of the necessary interdependence of all the ostensibly conflicting answers – a sense much fainter and more tentative here than in *The Aerodrome*, and offered as an abstract consolatory notion rather than a powerful and securely-grounded

metaphor. As an enquiry into typical conditions, and the infer-
ences to be drawn from them, *Why Was I Killed?* does have
moments reminiscent of, say, *Rasselas*. But although the soldier has
found some slight alleviation of his uneasiness in the very diversity
of response that he once thought so obstructive, in this conclusion
in which nothing is concluded the briefly gathered mourners are
sent back into the world alone, their experience not tutored into
the prospect of wisdom but disintegrating to its original state as
they leave the sanctuary.

The sequence Warner had by now established, whereby such
temporary accommodations as are reached in one novel are refined
or challenged by the next, was to progress one further stage. In
1945, not long after the pacification of the Greek civil war, he took
up the directorship of the British Institute at Athens. This must
certainly have been a privileged, and for a devoted classicist a
particularly poignant, situation from which to observe some of the
realities of the post-war settlement, reflections on which form the
basis of the last of his political allegories, *Men of Stones* (1949). The
setting of this novel, without being any more specific than before,
is clearly Balkan or Middle Eastern, at a point of uneasy intersection between the first and third worlds. The most prominent
moods are of naive or hectoring enthusiasm, and exhausted helplessness, alike emerging from the immediate aftermath of a conflict
which appears to demand of present affairs a stability bought at
any cost short of the final one. This condition serves as the new
frame within which Warner returns to old preoccupations, with
leadership, morality, faithlessness – the big themes which now
more explicitly acknowledge Dostoyevskian (and, more distantly,
Conradian) influences. Warner attempts here for the first time to
move beyond the experience of his own generation and their
immediate elders, and to match the arguments to younger characters who, in two cases in *Men of Stones*, have lived not merely
under conditions of ideological perplexity and imminent crisis, but
through extremes of violence, suffering and degradation which it
was their chief concern simply to survive. The novel also enters
new ground in anticipating to an extent the dispersal, to remote
and peripheral areas, of political difficulties and their accompanying utopian experiments which, with the defeat of Hitler, were no
longer central to the Western European consciousness. But despite
much striking material and promise, the book fails to consolidate

these advances; it falls back rather automatically on old habits of treatment in respect of subjects which it knows to be newly resistant to them. In doing so it raises starker questions about the limitations of its allegorical method, searching for images of order and clarity in a context that can no longer yield them; its efforts to suggest the kind of radical interconnection of apparent differences, that had contributed to much productive tension in *The Aerodrome*, seem here increasingly the jaded exercises of a blocked will.

The novel is organised around a familiar threefold clash; there is a demented idealist, an ineffectual liberal and a mystic. The idealist Leader in this case is the Governor of a barely-accessible island prison, who, Kurtz-like, takes advantage of his unrestrained power to indulge in experiments upon his subjects. The theory on which his practice is based claims history as a demonstration of how human beings only find happiness in religious faith or in voluntary submission to a higher power; the true benefactor of mankind must provide it with a new faith. Establishing himself as God entails his behaving in ways deliberately outrageous to secular judgement, treating humans as wholly dispensable, and supplying symbolic rationales for murderous and barbaric actions, including the killing of his father, his wife and the inhabitants of an entire village. The Governor is nominally under the jurisdiction of a government anxious to ingratiate itself with the Western powers, and a Mr Goat, a representative of English liberalism at its most parochial and protected, is sent by his cultural mission (a caricature British Institute) to produce a performance of *King Lear* on the prison battlements. Goat enters the scene like a knight of Romance eager for the test, and promptly embarks on an affair with the Governor's wife Maria; in the course of his preparations and rehearsals he becomes increasingly bemused by the events in which he is both caught and implicated. The second plot involves the search undertaken by Marcus, a concentration camp survivor, and an army veteran, Captain Nicholas, for a miraculous religious painting Marcus heard about in the camp, and which he thinks would, if found, secure his currently shaky belief that there is a spiritual dimension to life beyond the nihilism towards which his harrowing experiences have brought him. The two halves of the book meet when the Governor, acting on information unwittingly supplied by Goat, destroys the painting, as part of his attempt to extirpate all evidence of an effective religion besides his own. Marcus, deprived of the proof he had sought, nonetheless asserts his belief to be indestructible. At the concluding performance of *Lear*, Maria, in the role of Cordelia, is found to be really dead, murdered by her husband; this latest atrocity provides a pretext for government forces, fearful of the Governor's megalomaniac designs and their effect on public opinion abroad, to destroy him and initiate a fresh civil war, whose beginning Marcus and the other survivors can only blankly watch.

Clearly there is much in this outline that recalls *The Aerodrome*. The Governor invites immediate comparison with the Air Vice-Marshal, but in every respect appears the less substantial figure. He has a similar military bearing but none of the magnetism, personal or ideological, that could inspire uncertain youths to become his followers. Such cohorts as the Governor has look up to him not with the enthusiasm of those who see their own aspirations concentrated and aggrandised in his heroic figure, but from the despair of their utter subjection and dependence; it seems scarcely credible at the end of the novel that he should retain sufficient partisans to pose a serious threat. The fascistic movement at the aerodrome blended ideological conviction with material power; the cult of the élite group was founded on their tangible supremacy, as pilots or technicians of the future. The Governor by contrast has neither élite nor movement. He takes everything on himself, and makes merely personal gestures towards ideas that were previously social and typical. He deliberately kills his father on the grounds that 'by dissolving the most obvious link between oneself and the generations which have gone before one is, as it were, asserting one's free and chosen existence' (p. 125), but it is an action rather designed to increase the mystique surrounding his private character than as a symbolic revolutionary example. And while the dangerous attractiveness which the Air Vice-Marshal embodied could continue in different forms after his own had been circumvented, because of the tight relationship between supplanter and supplanted that his project was implicated in, the Governor's menace does not really extend beyond the limits of his authority. There is a certain chilling authenticity in the initial presentation of such chaotic post-war conditions as might well have allowed for the isolated emergence of such figures, exploiting positions of temporary impregnability, but the Governor has no technological organisation or military strength in league with his ideas; his is a world of secluded obsessions at the fringes of a culture which is only notionally challenged by them. There is in consequence a sense in this book, stronger if more intermittently realised than in the more orthodox science-fiction scenes of *The Wild Goose Chase*, of entering a space set apart for the metaphysical extension of certain otherwise covert ideological practices; a breakdown of convention so complete that the appalled and appalling speculations indulged here might appear to be perfectly normal. But in comparison with *The Aerodrome*, where the setting both supported the specific arguments of the book and aligned them with more general questions, about modernisation and rapid technological change, the alliance of the realistic and the abstract in *Men of Stones* is much more problematic. The more accurate the picture of the particular circumstances that support the Governor's experiment in power, the more it subverts the allegorical generalisations the book wants to draw from it; his tyranny seems already belated and impotent, tolerated for a while in the general post-war falling-off of concern, with meanness rather than warped grandeur at its core. Part Grand Inquisitor, part fugitive war criminal, the Governor stands as the last hideous outcome of the anxious idealism and contempt for 'low aims' which had motivated Warner's and others' pursuit, two decades earlier, of the truly strong man, the healer of a diseased culture, the caster-off of the stifling weight of the past. There is a dogged integrity, in many ways admirable, about Warner's thus dismantling the remnants of his former optimism, but the retractation denudes his central figure of much of its interest.

The novel was originally to have been called 'The Prison'. The change of title invites a change of emphasis, from the place and the fantasies indulged in it, towards the problems of responding to conditions which seem everywhere to advertise the moral and emotional helplessness of their observer. The opening pages provide a striking and ominous panorama of such new circumstances and their effect; there is a potent mixture of concise evocation and brittle satire of a kind which, unsure how to free itself from collusion in the attitudes it exposes, gratifies itself with occasional apologetic detonations:

> The prison is situated on an island of extraordinary beauty. Tourists who go past either by the railway on the mainland or by boat over the sea look upon it, in its brilliant setting of blue water, as a fine example of medieval architecture, which indeed it is. If anyone tells them that it is now a prison, they nod their

heads, as though that were to be expected. Then, perhaps, they turn their eyes to another direction, to the sweeping lines of the mountains which surround this land-locked bay and, below the mountains, to the green fringe of the coast and the folds of hills whose colours and outlines change with the changing daylight . . . There is no sound or stir in the air, except for the hawks that circle screaming about the battlements; though occasionally a fisherman who approaches the castle more nearly than is customary may hear a human voice uplifted in terror or in agony, for the prisoners are treated with an inhumanity which, in other days, would have excited universal disapprobation.   (pp. 11–12)

The writing, with a heavy-handed panache in many ways more appropriate than any great or energetic subtlety, continues to register in its tone the state it describes: the apathy and vague distress of people dully resigned to an enforced co-existence with things that remain, at some suppressed level, wholly abhorrent to them. A minister in the government, reminded in polite conversation of his reputation for savagery in the late war, would 'roar with laughter, as though what was past could always be regarded as, in some sense, humorous' (p. 14); the prisoners themselves are the focus of a more explicitly bleak summary of the collapse of political hope:

> In the unlikely event of their liberation, most of the prisoners would, no doubt, automatically rally to their various banners, and yet they would be uneasily conscious that those banners had, in the meantime, been redesigned: that the direction of march had been altered, that they themselves, though still conscious of the necessity for seeking power for their own groups, had lost any clear idea of the wider prospects for which this power, when acquired, was to be exercised.   (p. 13)

The general sense of lost 'prospects', taken with the related cases of Maria and Marcus, extends beyond the immediate issue of political goals to reopen the question *Why Was I Killed?* considered more abstractly, of those who have either been altogether deprived by history of the notional future which still awaited the characters of the pre-war fiction, or who have suffered in such ways as to make of that future largely a period of trying to continue as though nothing had happened. Much the strongest moments in *Men of*

Stones are those which dramatise or glimpse such people as they warily circle each other, groping for tolerably secure positions while the distant, incompatible attitudes that surround them flare up in sudden and rapidly-extinguished skirmishes.

The early stages of the relationship between Goat and Maria have something of this quality. The initial excitement is familiar in Warner; the naive young Englishman is seduced in a disarmingly blasé and offhand manner. In Goat's case, unlike George's in *The Wild Goose Chase*, there is the additional twist of his concern to pay a properly deferential liberal respect to the mysterious or imperfectly grasped foreign customs which are bullying him; there is a gulf between him and Maria which their relationship cannot cross and simply has to ignore. Warner gives a comic picture, which manages to be simultaneously affectionate and sour, of the extent to which Goat's upbringing has armed him for the battle of life – 'He even described to her, though this was a subject on which he was usually most reticent, his feelings at the time when he first won a championship in long-jumping' (p. 32) – promptly capped by the account of Maria's experiences among guerrillas. For Goat the opening of so great a divide is both bewildering and rather convenient, since by calling into question whether his own experience of the world could really provide a remotely secure base for the moral judgement of others, it enables him to rationalise inclinations which had previously caused him pangs of guilt – an affair that involves betraying his fiancée, or a view of the prison more concerned with its scenic potential for his *Lear* than with the activities of the regime. The relief, as much as the anxiety, that Goat is afforded, by the disintegration of the grid through which he had seen the world, touches the same psychological truth as in Roy's case, and adds powerfully here to the atmosphere of slackening moral attention which seems entailed by conditions too rapid and intractable to be stably absorbed. Hence the two lovers' awkward and frequently baulked approaches to each other appear emblematic of a more general search, alternately nervous and austere, among the ruins for something that at least resembles the intimacy it cannot actually be. But it is not long before the allegorical melodrama takes over, and the book attempts to resurrect the old pattern whereby mutual passion brings to light a hidden relationship between apparent strangers. Their initial estrangement was too authentic to respond to this treatment, and Maria's subsequent sentimental conversion to the redemptive

powers of love undermines what was most convincing and suggestive earlier – to the point where it seems that Warner's anxiety to find
something positive has led him to be false to his own perceptions.

A similar problem arises with the story of Marcus. His reflections
on his experiences in the camp are no less intense for their
avoidance of particular details, since his preoccupation is with the
prolonged exposure to such conditions, bringing about a loss of
humanity – either by a deliberate jettisoning or by an apparently
unavoidable process of erosion:

> We were gradually beginning to accept as part of the natural
> order things which, only a few months ago, would have
> profoundly horrified us. We could not avoid the question – was
> all this, the tortures, the savagery, the indifference, really the
> natural order? I don't mean merely were these things the most
> likely things to happen to us: obviously they were. What
> bothered my friend was the idea that perhaps these things in a
> way ought to be happening everywhere, that there was in the
> universe no sort of sanction for any other form of life.   (p. 80)

In this context the slightly unhinged deliberateness of his search
for the weeping picture seems a therapeutic concentration of
energy and will. The Governor for his part equally deliberately
destroys the picture, in the meantime razing the entire village
around it, as an expression of his omnipotence and divine arbitrari-
ness. But when Marcus finds that his quest has led only to another
atrocity, his energy seems to fizzle out. His protesting amid such
scenes the existence of 'love and pity', his sudden decision to
abandon the search for material evidence of them, appear rather
wilfully imposed upon a moment when the experience of such a
man as Marcus remains more difficult of access. He wants to assert
a spontaneous recognition that his former will to truth had been
misdirected, that he was 'guilty of having required too much assurance' (p. 154), and that the mystical revelation he now encounters can be only haltingly articulated, because all the resources
of linguistic order and coherence have been pre-emptively seized
by his enemy. But the argument turns the whole scene into an
allegory of Faith versus Reason, in a manner at odds with its
more convincing disclosures; these suggest not so much that
Marcus's reaction typifies the Christian response to evil, as that the
hardening process he underwent in the camp continues to exert

influence on a belief that leaves him almost complacently cut off from those on whose behalf he sought it. If one felt that his avowal was a private accommodation arising from obscure sources, it would have more strength and more pathos. As it is, the novel would clearly like to endorse it more generally, overlooking the more difficult idea, that such a position might be both gained and limited by his specific experiences as a camp survivor. Hence in respect of both these younger characters, who have lived through extreme suffering, the novel rather shies away from the challenge their real independence and inaccessibility poses. Instead of pursuing the Conradian confrontations it sets up, between widely-severed assumptions forced suddenly to examine themselves, *Men of Stones* recuperates more typical and conventional ideas and behaviour, and turns to an allegorical assertion of common ground – reinforced by the implicit parallels with *King Lear*, where Maria and Marcus play something like the roles of Cordelia and Edgar respectively.

The Governor had effectively stolen the language of rational description, in a chilling moment when he recounts to Marcus and the other appalled onlookers their own reactions to the atrocity he has just committed:

> "Captain Nicholas appears to be angry. He is a relic of the past, of those days when such phrases as 'moral indignation' had not entirely lost their meanings. The girl . . . is clearly in love and has eyes only for you. Though possibly she would not admit it, compared with her own feelings the destruction of a dozen families means little to her. The two old people, whom you see sitting on the ground moaning, have taken up an attitude which is entirely conventional. They have sat like this before and, no doubt, they expect to sit like this again. In a way their attitude is respectable, since they recognise the uncertainty of life, and the response they make to it, by time-honoured gestures, has, though it is out of date, a certain dignity."   (p. 146)

This is a flash of Warner at his best, still capable of landing on the reader some hard and unexpected blows. Derivations from Nietzsche and Dostoyevsky combine with the particular circumstances of this story to form in the Governor a rationalism wholly untrammelled, casting a shadow in which all other responses have subsequently to stand. Marcus's assertion of faith provided a suspiciously ready answer, but elsewhere the case might have to be met by strategies of indirection, since the direct reactions are so hard-put to defend themselves. It may be that the intention behind the novel's treatment of this central scene of horror and confrontation is to counter obliquely the supremacy of reason, which is otherwise answered only by the violent and confused exclamations of Captain Nicholas; to interpose a different order of apprehension, that resists despair and incoherence and goes on searching for ways to speak of what is conventionally called the unspeakable. George Steiner seemed to be suggesting, in the course of commentary on Benjamin, that this was a possible function of allegory; 'only allegory, in that it makes substance totally significant, totally representative of ulterior meanings and, therefore, "unreal" in itself, can render bearable an authentic perception of the infernal'.[3] In this respect, the allegorising of Good and Evil in *Men of Stones* may be an attempt to substitute an intellectual and aesthetic response for the immediately humane one whose faltering tenability the book is only too conscious of. But in practice it seems tired and perfunctory; the apparently climactic debate peters out and the scene of the razzia is quickly forgotten. The novel fails to find images arising from its own conditions that could effectively crystallise the problems it addresses; it falls back instead on its uneasy and ultimately dwarfing relationship with *King Lear* for them.

Goat's preparations for and eventual catastrophic performance of *Lear* touch on three related areas of concern. There is the simple parallel picked up in the novel's title, by which Marcus, Captain Nicholas and the cultural attaché Colonel Felson, roughly in the roles of Edgar, Kent and Albany, helplessly watch the working-out of an evil they can neither prevent nor adequately respond to. They should 'howl', in an expressive primal sympathy, but the gulf between themselves and what they see is too great. Related to this is a more muted question, running through the novel, about the implications of performing plays in, or otherwise taking steps to legitimise, such situations as this; from the tourists at the beginning to the disconcerted first-night audience at the end, the novel points up the kinds of deliberate indifference that have to be cultivated in order that life should continue at all. Felson, a caricature colonial administrator, is given one meditation which doubtless reflects Warner's own experience in his own not dissimilar role in Greece, resignedly acknowledging the structures of power which are currently holding down the lid on unreconciled conflicts, and which must on no account be disturbed:

> More important than all else was his simple directive – to be non-political . . . He would have once again, he reflected, to watch, with hardly even a show of disapproval, the working of a system most hostile to his dearest beliefs and a source of actual danger to his friends. (p. 208)

A third question introduced by way of *Lear* is considerably more difficult and ambitious; it asks whether art can have any kind of purchase on this reality in the first place. When Goat, acting Lear, realises that the 'body' he is carrying really is a body, the performance, of course, simply breaks down. The anticipated ritual appropriate to the staging of such a scene, whereby the words, however terrible, still have in their drive and rhythm an expressive power that might, by continuing to face the 'image of that horror', be the beginning of consolation, breaks down with it; the real events do not match the 'promised end'. The idea of this climax has a certain brutal strength, trying to push as far as it can into the question the Governor had asked: 'Which of your poets and philosophers and lovers would have imagined the final age, the age of the concentration camp and the atomic bomb?' (p. 150). But however hard *Men of Stones* tries to concentrate all the accumulated energies of its predicaments into the single tableau, the inverted Pieta of *Lear* which is to be both constructed and challenged, they have been effectively dissipated long before. The relationship between Goat and Maria, the image of whose destruction is supposed to carry all that symbolic weight, has lost the one thing that was convincing about it, so instead of tragedy the reader sees only the idea attached to the scene. The attempts elsewhere to pursue structural analogies with the play – the collapse of authority into competing factions, the mad 'trial' scene, the 'reconciliation' through love – are distributed too haphazardly around the novel ever to be more than tokens of a power it knows it cannot have. In its ambition to represent simultaneously the last fall of the curtain and the mind's inability to register it with any adequacy, *Men of Stones* has taken on far more than it can manage.

The question it aims to put, as to whether and how such disintegration of the human bond could be approached in art, did of course rapidly come to occupy a central position, almost a commonplace, in post-war works – often through the sanction it supposedly gave to much rhetorical posturing that claimed the authority of an experience it had not actually known. For those placed otherwise, such as actual camp survivors, the experience could emerge either in stark and unembellished testimony, as in some of Primo Levi's writings, for instance, or through the most complex transmutations of language and image in Paul Celan. For those who became the witnesses of others' suffering, a more conventional displaced Gothic might attempt to mediate, as I think it does in the writings of Mervyn Peake, between this actual shock and the literary manners in which shock used to register. In cases where the experience is wholly vicarious, the same kinds of challenge to subjectivity and pathos as are raised in Warner's book will occur; such works will always reflect, even where they fail to negotiate, a struggle for dominance between the event itself and the reaction to it. Perhaps Geoffrey Hill's poem 'September Song' [4] is as scrupulous as any such work, in addressing the concurrent needs to speak and to question one's right and ability to do so. The allegorical gestures in *Men of Stones* at least draw attention to some of these difficulties, even where they do not greatly illuminate them.

For the allegorical method here finally reaches, I think, the impasse which both *The Wild Goose Chase* and *The Aerodrome* had approached but had managed precariously to ward off. *Men of Stones*, subtitled 'a melodrama', tries to employ the same kind of machinery which had worked, in the tight microcosmic world of *The Aerodrome*, to suggest the common origins of disparate experiences; we learn for instance that the Governor and Marcus are brothers, and that Captain Nicholas knew Maria in the past. We see also the defeat of the Governor by the Minister's forces at the end as symbolically a case of Evil brought down not by Good but by a lesser and meaner evil. (Marcus refused to take part in the final overthrow, on the grounds that the Governor's ideas could only be genuinely defeated by other, stronger ideas; but in the specific situation of the novel, where the global settlement makes any such large-scale shift impossible, they would be more effectively defeated by precisely the continuing combination of widespread apathy, indifference and fragmentation they were designed to overcome.) But this machinery produces no clarifying or evocative effect, nothing of the 'grandeur or insecurity' Warner felt could be best expressed at the intersection of the real and the allegorical. It is a merely mechanical effort to rivet together things which remain authentically splintered. The differences which the allegory wishes to reconcile, the stances which it wishes to typify, are in this novel so extreme that to see fundamental connections entails a withdrawal from engagement of Olympian proportions; a retreat to an overview of things so high and distant from them that almost all differences are simplified or cancelled out, and the vantage-point is thus brought more than ever into tacit collusion with that of the totalitarianism it claims to expose.

Such questions as arise from the tendency of these novels' methods have provided much of interest and significance; there is always a surreptitious commentary by the fiction on the arguments with which it deals. In respect of the problem which *Men of Stones* finds, I think, insoluble, *The Wild Goose Chase* had found a provisional, if profoundly unsettled, accommodation. The impetus of its politics enabled it to regard extreme differences as only apparent, made so by a process of deliberate and oppressive mystification; the agency of the sceptical traveller could, despite manifold difficulties, aim to distinguish the necessary from the superfluous and reduce some of those differences back to manageable proportions. *The Aerodrome* had suggested that the power required to enforce such a re-ordering was too compromised, the patterns in which it was implicated too complex to be disentangled or overborne, and that the retreat to a form of liberal optimism was itself riddled with latent inconsistencies. In these cases the allegory could deepen the problems in the same moment as it sought to express them. But in *Men of Stones* the moves towards allegorical treatment of its materials seem to produce less meaning rather than more. Its situation is one where no single figure could hope either to maintain anything like George's mixture of engagement and detachment, or to unite as Roy had done the conflicts of his immediate world in his own personal development. Its literary parallels and the attitudinising of its sudden changes of heart run too often simply contrary to its perceptions rather than in stimulating tracery with them. An allegory of ideas in progress towards a central, ordering discovery – either forwards in the direction of a utopian future, or backwards into a revelation of origins – can no longer make any headway. Warner was now to abandon allegorical fiction altogether, and when he returned to the novel in 1958 it was with a study of Julius Caesar, one of the few figures in history who appeared to have achieved something of what was no longer achievable.

Notes

1. Edwin Muir, reviewing *Why Was I Killed?* in 'The Listener', 9
    December 1943, p. 674.
2. *Heraclitus: The Cosmic Fragments*, ed. Kirk, Cambridge 1954, p. 203.
3. George Steiner, introduction to Walter Benjamin's *The Origin of
    German Tragic Drama*, trans. Osborne, London 1977, p. 20.
4. Geoffrey Hill, 'September Song', from *King Log*, London 1968, p. 19.

6
The Historical Novels

The ambitiousness and guarded optimism with which Warner and his fellow-writers had begun their careers seemed finally to dwindle away in the atmosphere of lowered horizons and anxiety not to be fooled which rather characterised the 1950s – and which, incidentally, exerted such a powerful retrospective influence on subsequent critical views of the 1930s. With the exception of the 'entertainment novel' *Escapade* (1953), in which he attempted to burlesque his own allegorical methods in a wry acknowledgement of their newly-inappropriate portentousness, Warner altered the course of his literary career and concentrated on translation from the classics. Thucydides and Plutarch offered a more secure canvas on which he could trace the same interests – power, the relationship of individual and mass, the motive force of ideas, the dynamic progress of history – for which comparable models were no longer available in the contemporary world. The subsiding during the Cold War of revolutionary energies in the West, the entry into a period of lull, enabled Warner to take a more broadly historical view than hitherto of his formative years, whereby they might appear less as the final advance which old hopes had been pinned on, than as a particularly urgent phase in a continuing cycle of advance and recession; certainly, his general interpretation of history according to pre-Socratic codes of rhythm and balance becomes increasingly emphatic, until he has the weakest of his novels, *Pericles the Athenian* (1963), narrated by a particularly self-important and long-winded Anaxagoras.

His work as a translator and teacher of classics had brought him back to fiction in 1958 with the first volume, *The Young Caesar*, of a two-part 'autobiography' of Julius Caesar. *Imperial Caesar* (1960) was followed by *Pericles* and finally *The Converts* of 1967. Each of these novels is set in a crucial period of the development of the ancient West: respectively, the foundation of the Roman imperiate, the establishment of Athenian democracy, and the gradual ascendancy, reflected in the career of St Augustine, of Christianity in the Roman world. The search in these works is for an instrument broadly similar to the earlier allegories, whereby the period could be investigated through the experiences of characters whose private conflicts somehow embodied the general passion, although only in *The Converts* does Warner utilise a wholly fictitious narrator to this end. In the other novels his method is not to surround an imaginary story with authentic period detail, but scrupulously to reconstruct a known history through the eyes of one deeply involved in it. The actual events themselves and the speculations they give rise to are held to constitute sufficient interest; Warner allows himself almost nothing by way of incidental embellishment or license. So while an immediate model for his *Caesar* novels was Robert Graves's *Claudius*, Warner's work is altogether colder and more austere. It has none of the obviously popular features of the Graves; neither the mix of court intrigue, sex and violence, nor the appeal (so importantly an element in the post-First War flavour of Graves's books) of the alternative, controversial, insider's challenge to the authorised version of history – the last laugh, as it were, of the despised and disregarded at the expense of the supposedly powerful. Warner even denies himself the luxury of any dialogue, beyond a few remarks famously or rhetorically attributed to the real characters he draws upon; he stays wholly within the compass of Caesar's mind as it produces an apologia for the life, resembling here a disinterested appraisal, there a Roman *Mein Kampf*. Placing the fictional project under such extreme constraints entails quite different imaginative tasks from those faced by the allegorist. There is no longer any scope for symbolic inventions which could organise and simplify the material into a discernible shape. If the narrator, bereft of opportunities for allegorical expression, wishes to interpret historical events in allegorical terms, he becomes enmeshed in the partiality of his own account. On a number of occasions in the *Caesar* novels Caesar himself raises the question of whether it is the outcome of a sequence of events which alone permits a pattern to be detected in them; and, since he is himself the 'outcome', what value can be attached to his deterministic interpretations. In this case, for all his admission of imponderables, Caesar remains effectively convinced of precisely what it would be in his interest to say anyway – that the times he lived in conspired to produce him and insisted on the necessity of his triumph. The problem for the novelist using such a narrator is to construct a world and a purchase on it which allows for the possibility of others without ever departing from its own; to create for the reader a further space, accessible through gaps and tangents in the text where ironies can operate beyond the narrator's control. The virtues of Caesar's outlook are clear, and clearly endorsed by Warner; the shortcomings are more subtly interwoven. But there is still, beneath the straightforward epic narrative, a vestige of the interplay between the didactic material and the form containing it which had provided the further life and interest of Warner's earlier works; there are prompted reflections upon how a history is constructed, which arise quite generally and with none of the self-conscious flourishing of sabotage familiar in many novels of the 1960s and 1970s which use history to explore fictionality. (Not that the narrative is devoid of evocative and piquant occasions for such reflections; at one point the consul Bibulus attempts to obstruct Caesar's advance to power by the legal technicality of suspending Senate business for a year in order to 'watch for omens'.) It is unfortunate that in the two last novels this extra quality is almost entirely absent, and the author's disengagement from his material becomes deadening, but the *Caesar* novels offer numerous satisfactions.

As Caesar embarks upon the account of his life, the writing carefully sustains, for long periods, the illusion of a timeless rationalism, speaking across the centuries. The historical distance appears to be virtually cancelled, while a flattering intimacy is created between narrator and reader. There is a bond, a tacit assumption as by sceptical men-of-the-world, that the things which constitute the habits and conventions of their respective times can be picked up or discarded as they please; the fully adult mind can recognise the influence such things exert over others, and the political uses to which this recognition can be put, while itself remaining free to move in and out of that culture at will. This appeal to a reservoir of shared understanding enables Warner's Caesar to voice a number of opinions which bear upon his author's consistent preoccupations; 'People cannot live without efficiency, but they are not prepared to die for it', for example (*The Young Caesar*, p. 159), or:

> Few men ever fully grow up. From youth to old age they will always demand an assurance that cannot be found in their own natures. And this demand for assurance will, of course, become particularly urgent during periods of history when a society is obviously not living in accordance with its own pretensions.
> (*Imperial Caesar*, p. 14)

The world of Warner's youth now lies in the light of a more completely disinterested view than any taken in the allegorical novels. Indeed, for much of the time such blunt realism makes Caesar sound rather like a more assured narrator of *The Professor*:

> Cicero ... was already beginning to see in himself an idealised version of some great statesman from ancient history, curbing what was extreme, guiding what was good and loyal by the sheer force of integrity and a deserved prestige. He had not yet begun to realise that he had neither a party nor a programme, that he was rapidly losing the goodwill of the people, and that the support now given to him by the nobility would melt away as soon as some new situation arose in which the real factors of our history were more clearly revealed.
>
> (*The Young Caesar*, pp. 232–3)

(A nice touch, that a Roman should regard the Greeks as 'ancient history'.) Caesar is also granted accurate prevision of his own fate and the fates of others, all helping to fill out the portrait of wisdom, experience, farsightedness. The remarkably level tone of this writing does so much to establish familiarity that the reader can be quite disturbed by sudden reminders of his real alienation from Caesar's world and its assumptions. Sometimes a particular detail culled from Plutarch will be deftly inserted in a passage of otherwise neutral reflection, as when Caesar recalls the opening of Pompey's theatre, where 500 lions and 400 panthers had been killed in spite of the 'strange behaviour' of the crowd, who 'appeared for once to sympathise with the sufferings of the wild animals' (*Imperial Caesar*, p. 109). More often, since the Roman scene is being observed by one to whom its details are sufficiently familiar never to need mentioning, the very evenness of a style so unencumbered by conventional reference-points of dialogue or local colour can fascinate almost to giddiness. Thus we hold on to a notion of Caesar's humanity and generosity of spirit in the midst of his considering, for example, whether it would be to his advantage to have his prisoners executed at once or after a slight delay; or his complacent reminiscence of having an entire Gallic tribe sold into slavery – 'I was told that the number was 53,000' (*Imperial Caesar*, p. 77). Warner's best writing was always able to challenge the reader with a sense of the size of the world, a glimpse behind the words of much larger things than are ostensibly related in them.

There are two crucial periods in the formation of Caesar's career and outlook. The first is his experience as a terrified youth during the civil wars between Marius and Sulla; the second his sudden realisation, after his victory over the Helvetii some 30 years later, that he could go on to conquer the whole of Gaul and unite it under Roman rule. From this latter point his steady acquisition of power becomes increasingly directed to particular goals, and his subsequent re-reading of his earlier life proceeds to emphasise those elements which support the idea of a consistent purpose. His dream was to introduce into life 'a principle of order, a new direction discovered', that will 'continue to the end of time' (*The Young Caesar*, p. 61) – a grand passion qualified by his recognising

the full squalor, the confusion, the hypocrisy, the savagery, the demeaning beastliness of political activity. Indeed no time could have been more propitious for making these discoveries than were the most impressionable years of my life, those from the age of fifteen to that of twenty. (*The Young Caesar*, pp. 60–1)

Even so, the full influence upon him of the events of his adolescence is perhaps never completely acknowledged. His first experiences of public life in Rome were so far removed from the idea of 'Rome' evoked by the republicans that he regarded them with a contempt and an intolerance which, if anything, increased as he moved closer to establishing the conditions for their ultimate defeat. The competing factions in the civil wars were associated in his young mind with the personalities of their leaders rather than the policies they promoted, partly because of his family connection with Marius, partly because the policies were effectively buried for long periods under the fog of individual rivalry and vengeance. Hence his view of historical development inevitably placed great emphasis on the roles of the leading men: 'Events seem to have been centred in and reflected by great personalities' (*The Young Caesar*, p. 188). He qualifies this by remembering that 'there has been, as it were, an undercurrent of more final importance than those characters, and scarcely perceived by any of them', but this perception still supports his demand that power should be concentrated in the hands of a single individual. His demand is not for a policy issuing from and administered by institutions run collectively, but for a revolution directed by one man's will, 'the transformation of the whole scene into something different' (p. 188). Clearly

Caesar grew up during a period when the Roman political balance had shifted decisively in favour of personal aggrandisement. Marius had unwittingly established new conditions by enlisting the poor into his legions for the Numidian wars of 108 BC, so creating a professional army whose primary loyalty was to its commander rather than to Rome. Sulla had been the first to take advantage of this situation by using his own army to seize Rome itself, incidentally demonstrating how readily the new soldiers could be induced to switch their allegiances, and convincing the young Caesar that a popular and adroit army commander was now the only figure who really counted for anything. Such conditions allowed a potential freedom of manoeuvre for ambitious individuals hardly matched in Western history, and certainly only with extreme difficulty by twentieth-century ideologues.

Caesar was, of course, no ideologue; those with coherent political theories counted him as their enemy, and it was the unpredictable and unstable in him rather than any consistent view which attracted attention. In his early years his ambitiousness served a mixture of adventurism and dignitas, a sense of what was due to him, and only later did he arrive at a more radical political programme. But when he did come to consider what might be achieved, and what factors would bear upon achievement, his thinking, as Warner presents it, was dominated by the impact upon him of the great figures of his youth, Marius, Sulla and Sertorius. He is primarily concerned to make these men into symbols of the range of possibility it might lie in his own power to emulate or correct, but the reader also suspects a deeper fascination, a more romantic vision of ancestry or ancient glory, than the brisk and pragmatic assessments allow for. These three have all the colour of the past; none of Caesar's own contemporaries, of whatever stature, is able to evoke such complexity of response in him, as they are all seen merely as instruments or obstacles on his own route to power. Thus he regards Marius, for example, for all his thuggishness and political incompetence, as not just the leader of a popular movement but as the embodiment of popular aspirations. There is nothing noble or austere about this Roman grandeur; Marius is cunning, vindictive, manipulative, but incapable of deep hypocrisy or of dividing himself from his own actions. He remains faithful to what he is deemed to share with the plebeians, for which they not only forgive but admire and encourage his flamboyant excesses; for Warner's Caesar, Marius was a symbol

and example of that great force within the people itself which,
though nearly always dissipated, misdirected, distorted or
deceived, still exists and, in the last resort, controls events.

                                        (*The Young Caesar*, p. 172)

Caesar himself will eventually lose touch with the very force he
so clearly identifies. But it is important for him to envisage a kind
of leader who rides the tide and gathers into himself its vital and
progressive energies. It is a view which allows Sulla to be equally
firmly established in the demonology – firstly as Marius's antitype,
and then as Caesar's own. For once Marius is identified with what
is alive and growing in history, Sulla, an incomparably more astute
character, falls neatly into place as the epitome of repression,
negativity and perversion. It was, however, the uncontrollable
savagery during Marius's return from exile, rather than anything
perpetrated by Sulla, that made an 'indelible' impression on the
young Caesar, convincing him that 'all dignity, and with it the
possibility of affection, comes from restraint, whether self-imposed
or enforced from outside' (*The Young Caesar*, p. 72). It is typical of
Warner that he should thus quietly locate the seeds of his hero's
authoritarianism and coldness in a moment of revulsion from the
very man he is most attracted to.

Sertorius is a figure sufficiently distant to offer no resistance to
Caesar's appropriation of him. He is regarded as a kind of herald of
the greatness to come, a man who saw further than his contemporaries – 'he and I alone seem to have understood the history of our
times' (*The Young Caesar*, p. 64) – and who by being assassinated
exemplified some of the perils of foresight. To 'understand'
history, for Caesar, is to grasp that events have a necessary
direction, that changes have to be accepted and accelerated rather
than resisted; Sertorius's understanding, when governor of Spain,
was that the future success of Roman rule depended less on further
military conquests than on the gradual conversion of the subject
peoples into Romans. Since he was murdered by jealous inferiors
before 'the precise opportunity suited to his genius' (p. 156) could
present itself, the narrative at this point raises some easy ironies
(Caesar's story is told on the eve of the Ides of March); the career
and fate of Sertorius become the source of Caesar's vision of
durability, of the triumph of ambition over time. The key is to
ensure that the impact of one's deeds is irreversible; in Caesar's
case to establish the imperial idea so forcibly that even opposition

to it has to be voiced in its terms. Hence he deems that the only foreign enemy to have given him serious trouble, Vercingetorix, did so not merely through his military skills but because he appealed, as Caesar himself would have done, to the idea that his country was only viable as a unified State under a supreme commander. Caesar is not concerned to give a true account of Vercingetorix's position; the argument rests on an assumption of power so complete that it shifts the terms in which power can be discussed.

This was the supremacy which Sulla never enjoyed, although of the three great figures of Caesar's youth he was the only one who actually became dictator and established his own form of government in Rome. Trying to explain the mystery of Sulla's abdication, Caesar suggests that a moment of humiliation by Pompey revealed to Sulla his failure to solve the central political problem, which was not finally disposed of until the time of Augustus: how to prevent not only oneself but one's entire system of order from being overthrown by the same means one had used to secure it. Sulla's chagrin must have hardened into cynical disregard: 'To him what was important was that his own will had found its own expression in his own lifetime. The future, so far as he was concerned, could look after itself' (*The Young Caesar*, p. 120). The implicit distinction here between negative and positive dictatorship is essentially that made by Caudwell in his essay on T. E. Lawrence[1]; Sulla, like Hitler, was a 'false' hero, exploiting the same play of forces as his 'true' counterpart, Caesar or Lenin, but in reactionary and despairing directions. (This is not the only occasion when Warner's Caesar aligns himself with Marxist attitudes *avant la lettre*; of his unabating impulse to expand his realm he remarks 'in this necessity I find my freedom' (*The Young Caesar*, p. 302)). Caesar knows that the relationship between Sulla and himself is rather more complex than this; he is forced to follow the road which his rival both opened up and made more difficult by his abuses. Sulla is the character who most relentlessly haunts Caesar's imagination, and from whom in every respect he is most anxious to be distinguished. His first experience of the thrill of power came with his challenging Sulla in the street as a nine-year-old boy; and their second confrontation, after Caesar's marrying against the dictator's wishes, is deliberately exaggerated into a critical and symbolic moment:

It is possible, however, that Sulla, with his rare gift of intuition, may, during his long scrutiny of my face, have recognised the presence of powers of which I myself was unaware, and may, in his perverse and superstitious way, have respected them. Some such an explanation as this seems to be required to account for the fact that my life was spared.   (*The Young Caesar*, pp. 98–9)

(The rather dry and meticulous prose of this extract, a legacy of his work as a translator, is fairly typical of Warner's late writings.) Caesar's idea here is highly tendentious, completely discounting the intercessionary role of his powerful friends who swayed the judgement; he presents instead a more composed picture, to articulate that obscure anxiety about hidden forces which besets him whenever his reflections lead him to justify the holding of supreme power. It is clear to the reader, moreover, that the greater part of Caesar's ruminations upon kingship and divinity arise, unnoticed by him, in connection with thoughts of Sulla. While Sulla was seen as 'perverse and superstitious', 'claiming for himself some supernatural power', and thus 'showing an arrogance unprecedented in Roman history' (p. 98), the attribution of divine powers to their monarchs by Oriental peoples raises a different question: 'Was this, I wondered, a regression to a more primitive and superstitious past, or was it an enlightened recognition of the necessities of the modern world?' (*The Young Caesar*, p. 105). The question that had been asked despairingly of the Governor in *Men of Stones* can here be presented more positively. Caesar experiences a kind of erotic fascination with the legend of his own divinity, and with the unrestricted power absolute rulers wield, and in a fearful recoil from that consciousness he becomes over-insistent on the rational basis of kingship. Hence *his* intention, in 44 BC, to adopt the title of King, is a piece of considered statecraft opposed by the ignorant and sentimental; while Sulla, who might indeed have called himself King for merely self-indulgent reasons, is regarded ever more fiercely as the type of barbarous tyranny Caesar's enemies are stupidly attributing to himself.

Much of Caesar's increasing intolerance, as his power continues to grow, seems to derive from his suppressing, as something disorderly and superfluous, that element in his nature which responded ambivalently to the powers others enjoyed or exerted. But since the world no longer contains a power to rival his own, its part is to submit, rather than to distract him from his task with alternatives which he can now regard only as trivial or obsolete. He does admit to a difficulty in understanding why, since men are on the whole rational creatures, they are so reluctant to accept one greater than themselves patiently pointing out to them the rational course; as he says of his ordering the mutilation of recalcitrant Gallic prisoners at Uxellodunum, 'it was a savage punishment . . . but I was justly, I think, infuriated by the inability of these people to follow the logic of events' (*Imperial Caesar*, p. 181). To 'follow the logic' also entails accepting that Caesar's 'active star', like Cromwell's in Marvell's 'Horatian Ode', requires constant replenishment of opportunity; hence his eagerness, at the time of his assassination, to embark on a fresh war in Parthia so soon after so much bloodshed – a project that arouses only muted enthusiasm among the people the example of Marius should have taught him to respect.

His highhandedness and irascibility persist in spite of his efforts to justify them in terms of the deference due to his greatness. They can give to his assessments of his contemporaries a peremptory authority, proper to the man of action who is called upon to weigh up rapidly the relevant qualities of a likely opponent; these fundamental insights which emergencies provoke, insights upon which all more leisurely inspections of character are founded, recall the allegorical simplifications of character in Warner's early novels. Of Cicero, for example, Caesar remarks that while he constantly proclaimed the virtues of peace, the oratorical skills which alone secured his power could only be effective in conditions the reverse of peaceful; Cicero relied upon terror and hysteria continuing, so that he could regularly claim to have calmed them down. But this kind of decisive judgement runs into problems with those characters who struggle against the frame the 'realist' would put round them. Cato, Caesar's most implacable enemy, draws out his most vehement scorn. He is goaded almost to bemusement by Cato's obduracy; he is unsure whether to say of him that he represented something real but outdated, or something perennially false and corrupt. At one point he argues that Cato was not insincere:

> He genuinely believed in himself as an example of ancient virtue. This made him all the more troublesome and unnecessary; he could not grasp the fact that he was not living in antiquity, and, in the name of ancient virtue, he obstructed every demand that was made upon him by modern times.
>
> (*The Young Caesar*, p. 226)

Quite soon afterwards, however, Caesar changes tack, talking instead of Cato's 'affectation of what he imagined to have been the ancient virtues – an affectation so consistent and intense as almost to deserve the name of sincerity' (p. 254). Caesar commandeers the language of virtue for his own use, and opposition to his will that may, as for the Gallic captives, have honest motives, is presented not only as an 'unnecessary' obstruction to modernisation, but as a hypocritical fanaticism, a petulant refusal to admit to self-evident truths. (A comment on this might have been in order from the Belgic tribe of the Eburones, if a survivor were to be found, since Caesar caused them to be totally exterminated on the grounds that they had 'treacherously' attacked him, in a forlorn attempt to regain their liberty.) But he detests Cato most for the influence he has over Brutus, whom Caesar loves almost as a son. For all the radical differences between the ideas of freedom offered by the two dictators, the conversations of Caesar and Brutus have at times the accents of a more secure and amenable Air Vice-Marshal talking to Roy:

> 'There is something,' he said, 'which I call "liberty", and which I admit is difficult to define. Will any amount of efficiency and happiness make up for the loss of it?' At this moment I felt much affection for the young man. He was expressing himself in a doctrinaire manner; for this 'liberty' in our days, if understood to mean the unrestricted and irresponsible play of established forces in Roman politics, had led not only to inefficiency and unhappiness but to a state of affairs where, through insecurity, only rich men and soldiers were capable of exercising any kind of liberty of choice in ordinary affairs . . . Yet, still, what he said was true. There is a kind of liberty, dependent in part on political institutions, which is so valuable that, without it, life would not be worth living. I thought . . . that I might have convinced Brutus that I understood the meaning of this kind of liberty at least as well as he did.   (*Imperial Caesar*, p. 304)

Caesar would regard the Air Vice-Marshal as too dangerously close to Cato and Brutus, all three believing themselves to be 'greater than the power they exercise' (*Imperial Caesar*, p. 302), and thus too arrogant to take the steps necessary to ensure that their organisations survived them. But beyond his bland assumptions of understanding there remains the rankling lure of rebelliousness, a sense of the cost of Caesar's achievement; and while he recognises what he deplores, that some people will from sheer depth of conviction act in ways which the 'realist' finds absurdly reckless and self-indulgent, what perhaps he never quite grasps is that the existence of such people might be as fundamentally necessary to progress as his own.

He identifies the appeal of Cato as being essentially 'religious' (*Imperial Caesar*, p. 348). As Warner presents him, Caesar has always been aware of the unpredictable forces of devout belief and their dangerous influence in the State. But he shows no sign of ever imagining a time when religious enthusiasm might become so conjoint with State power as to make his own speculations, about the various cults and the historical needs they serve, seem seditious freethinking. He admires the official religion of Rome because its rites are propitiatory; the intention is not to obtain aid from the gods, but to prevent them from making volatile interventions in a world which humans could manage much better undisturbed. In this respect he anticipates his successors' attitudes towards the early Christians, who refused to fulfil what were seen as their civic obligations. But certain ideas which were already stirring in his disputes with the republicans, and which will become increasingly prominent as the Christian dispensation expands – such as passive heroism, or the claims of the contemplative over the active life – cannot but seem to Caesar puerile and frivolous. Still more would he be perplexed by a doctrine of conversion, which presented a suddenly new form and direction for a man's entire being. This conceptual limit is paradoxically one of the many advantages which Caesar has over the kinds of modern dictator Warner considered in his allegories; the latter, however atheistic themselves, still have to proceed against a Christian background which has infiltrated their own modes of thinking, leading them to call for a spontaneous reconstruction not only of the State but of man himself, of a kind Caesar never envisages. He in his turn suffers some of the disadvantages of the kind of wisdom he expounds – the self-delusion of the 'realist' who, again like a slightly more humane version of the Governor in *Men of Stones*, imagines that he can distil from his experiences a utilitarian schedule of man's needs and then provide for them. His increasingly disengaged calculations of the effects and values of different kinds of behaviour – 'I was ready at any time, if I could see therein a real possibility of advantage, to behave with mercy and with moderation', for example (*Imperial Caesar*, p. 158) – display the hardening, into something mechanical or monolithic, of what began spontaneously in his youth; the price of power becomes a similar shrinking of the spirit to that *The Wild Goose Chase* had encountered, once it sought to present its triumph as that of rational order over lesser and meaner things. In his lectures at Storrs, Connecticut, Warner was fond of pointing out how great a difference there was between the actual personality of the historical Caesar, feared above all for his speed and vitality, and the doctrine of Caesarism which derived from his success, all inflexible rigidity and unvarying decree; something of that conflict between self and system seeps into the narrative once the great challenges are past and fresh ones have to be invented.

Hence Caesar's political project, of authoritarian order as the basis of true liberty, consorts with the allegorical project of Warner's earlier writings. The selective imposition of patterns on the phenomena, tracing for them a necessary direction, enables them to mean more than was apparent at the time, and thus recovers true liberty from the threat of anarchy or flux, by relating particular experience to the general play of those hidden forces which can suddenly crystallise onto the surface. Such marshalling into order not only reveals the significance of things otherwise formless, but attempts, as the medieval allegorists had done, to delimit the extent of their significance, to hold them under the yoke of willpower, to allow for a detached appraisal which could control the anxieties it simultaneously disclosed. The allegorical project, as it developed through Warner's first five novels, always sought a balance between acknowledging the intricacy of what was expressed, and reducing that intricacy to manageable proportions in the moment of expression; just so in the development of Caesar's career, as the increasing aloofness and supremacy of the single view over its alternatives eventually produces a totalising order which has lost sight of its partiality or exclusiveness. In one respect the endless rhythms of this process can be laid out for inspection much more effectively on the canvas of the Roman world, since the absence of any conceivable nostalgia for such times allows for a more fully rational and abstract consideration of their course; at the same time the reader misses much of the urgency of feeling that had basted the intellectual meat of the novels which had contemporary settings.

In *Pericles the Athenian* this loss is much greater. The hero's already shadowy life is narrated by the philosopher Anaxagoras, whose own fussy and pedagogic nature merely distances his subject still further. Here the history that is told gains very little from being 'fictionalised'; the novelistic dimension simply provides Warner with an opportunity to expound at considerable length the various pre-Socratic theories that had always interested him, and to view the Pelopennesian war as a demonstration of certain universal principles – Athens expanding and in motion, Sparta standing still, and the like. But the narrator gets in the way of any prospect of our extrapolating these ideas to other circumstances by pedantically insisting that we should. The large-scale generalisations have given Warner a way of talking about ideas and issues in ways that obviate the need to make them concrete and embodied in action or in image; the result is an efficient historical reconstruction almost completely devoid of the productive interplay between method and material that helped vitalise the latter and protect it from staleness.

Much the same, unfortunately, is true of *The Converts*. For this novel Warner invents a narrator, Alypius, who recounts his passage from youth to maturity in terms of his relationship with his friend Augustine's gradual progress towards Christian faith. Alypius grows into a recognition of how the Roman world which had seemed so immutable is actually fragmenting, while still providing the only familiar forms of security or expectation, and thus setting its citizens at odds with their own perceptions. The convention of the Bildungsroman enables the implicit parallels, towards which all these historical novels faintly gesture, between their periods and Warner's own inter-war youth, to be pointed up more sharply. The anxious quest for assurance, the experimenting with various rival beliefs, the sudden rash of conversions, all speak of what Alypius describes as the lack of any consensus as to the view taken or the judgement passed on the world – an uncertainty which allows, as it did in Roy's case, for the enactment in the fluctuating moods of the individual of the more widespread discontents. But it is clear that Warner is now working with a very distant memory of his own growing pains. In his concern to present the earnest worries of youth he loses all sense of humour or irony, that half-acknowledged touch of the ridiculous which leavened the priggishness of his earlier heroes. In both *Pericles* and *The Converts* the main character is presented with quite uncritical admiration and reverence, in order that nothing should tarnish the idea of what he represented; and the vitality that once lay open to

glimpses beneath the broad wash of generalisation has now almost
completely dried up. Warner falls back increasingly mechanically
on a habit he was always prone to but which had in earlier books
retained its links with real meaning: the use of triplicate abstractions to describe effects. Augustine, for example, found Ambrose's
preaching

> less varied, less fanciful and perhaps less charming than the
> language of Faustus whom he had listened to in Carthage; but
> on the other hand there was a force, a sincerity and a simplicity
> which Faustus lacked.   (p. 183)

At times, as in parts of *The Aerodrome*, this way of writing had
seemed earned, a kind of relaxation after the stress of aiming for a
greater precision than the material could bear without unaccept-
able moral and political consequences. The very vagueness of the
terms, the latitude they could give to interpretation, marked a
partial retreat from the will to dominate and a move instead
towards a more impersonal and classical proportion. Now, however, the technique has become routine and Parnassian, adopted
as a substitute for engagement rather than a representation of a
stage which engagement had reached. As with *Pericles*, Warner's
concern not to intrude anything specious or distracting upon his
historical fidelity leaves much of the intrinsic interest of his
material short-changed; we are presented with a demonstration of
how something evolved, without ever being brought close enough
to the flaws and hesitations that really marked its evolution. And
where *The Converts* does deal lucidly with the issues which always
preoccupied him, it produces rather a monument to his views than
a fresh exploration of them.

Note

1.   Christopher Caudwell, *Studies in a Dying Culture*, London 1938, p. 31.

Afterword

In his essay on Dostoyevsky, published in 1946, Warner remarked that 'a really thorough investigation of the sick spirit . . . cannot be made without some sympathy with the sickness' (*The Cult of Power*, p. 40). A merely aloof or forensic survey will not work; the imagination of sympathy has to be engaged, in ways it may not fully control. Warner's point neatly identifies the main subject of his own work – the conflict of political ideas, and the emotional and psychological disturbances such ideas both express and answer to. Once that identification is made, however, and the nature simplified of what had been a creative exploration of grey and uncertain areas, the work can lose a good deal of its personality, becoming more of an illustration of a set thesis than a fresh adventure. 'The perpetual tension . . . between the rebel and the official', each 'contained in the same person' (*The Cult of Power*, p. 133), appears from *Why Was I Killed?* onwards to be the explicit subject with which the novels begin, rather than the discovery they more or less consciously arrive at. The problem of how much its material requires a fictional rendition in order to be fully achieved is one which the 'novel of ideas' has always to confront. And just as allegory was held in a certain contempt under the Romantic dispensation, so the term 'novel of ideas' has increasingly come since Warner's day to indicate something drearily naive or presumptuously importunate, academic and mechanical, altogether beneath the level of serious literature. It is often routinely assumed that the 'ideas' no longer have any interest for the contemporary reader, and that the 'novel' is merely an inert peg on which to hang them. But in the strongest examples of the genre, the ideas are put to sterner tests by the reader's full experience of the novel which contains them than might be the case were they presented essayistically. In Warner's attempts to dramatise the impact of ideas upon conduct in the world, the fiction need not be wholly 'realistic' in order to introduce shades and nuances lying outside an abstracted explanation. The author's failure to prevent all his artistic resources from gathering their own momentum can enhance rather than vitiate what he intends to say, by coming to provide a running critique, a vitalising revaluation of the ideas themselves, even in the midst of the most overt demonstrations of them.

Warner attempted to use allegorical structures and imaginary settings to disentangle what he felt to be the truly significant relations between individuals, relations lying beneath the veneer of the modern world's impenetrability. In so doing he and some of his contemporaries were struggling, with limited success, against the predominant distrust of general discussion within novels which grew up with early twentieth-century Modernism, and which has always been loath to acknowledge its own historical character. But there have been some signs in contemporary writing of an increasing interest in parabolic or utopian narrative forms not unlike those Warner explored, in which invention mingles with diagnostic commentary, and action is endowed, however tentatively, with allegorical meaning. Some takes a form similar to that which Robert Scholes some years ago called 'fabulation', where the main emphasis is on the design of the work and its deployment of linguistic resources; some has been called 'magic realism', an intertwining of naturalistic and symbolic modes particularly suited to the problematic juxtapositions of a Western colonial legacy and that of indigenous cultures in the Third World. (I mentioned à propos *Men of Stones* Warner's partial anticipation of the dispersal, into remote corners, of some of the political and moral problems that no longer seemed preoccupying in the West; the most cursory glance at the story of a Dr Bakhtiar, or a Dr Van Zyl Slabbert, might suggest how parochial it would be to assume that the 50-year-old arguments of *The Professor*, for example, had been conclusively decided.) Much of this modern writing is constructed around an ironic self-questioning, or self-recommending, of a kind Warner never indulges; his novels express no embarrassment as to the reality of the issues they address, nor evasiveness about their capacity to address them. Perhaps contemporary distrust of the humanism that Warner's kind took for granted, even while they quarrelled with and extended it, has gone too deep for an approach towards meaning as straightforward as his to be easily recovered. That straightforwardness might appear now to be merely the bewildered cry of the plain man, striking out in facile resentment against the intractability of things – an intractability which tends often to be seen, not as an idea peculiar to its period, but as the type of all knowledge.

But the allegorical vision, whereby isolated details find their place in a large connecting pattern – as with the airman's view of the fields – ideally complements rather than supersedes the labourer's more difficult view of the same scene. Allegorical vision is a provisional means to enlightenment, which cannot be maintained indefinitely. The memory of it has to be carried back down to the undulating land whose secrets are not so readily yielded. Such order as allegory discloses remains momentary and unstable; when fixed into a secular settlement of language or of politics which would deny its provisionality, it becomes over-reachingly totalitarian. For Warner, those dictators who see only the patterns which their wills impose, while ignoring the local constrictions, are figures not tragic but irreligious. They do not struggle against God, and thereby tacitly acknowledge his authority; they replace him with a fantasy of themselves which suppresses the division within them between the airman and the labourer – the two aspects whose interdependence is the source of all progress and all frustration. In *The Wild Goose Chase* and *The Professor* the strong-minded and decisive sons rebelled against all that was corrupt and indeterminate in the thinking of their fathers; but by the time of *The Aerodrome* and *Men of Stones* such hope as accrued came rather from the sons' rejection of their fathers' organised designs. And that rejection, so clearly rooted in the course of real history, could itself only be partial in novels such as these, since the allegorical methods which expressed it pulled back towards the very order that was put into question. It was this that provided the writing with an interest very different from the self-reflexive interventions and paradings of doubt by which so much modern fabulation reveals its loss of confidence. Where Warner is most successful his material works out its own distrust of its radical ambitions without recourse to games or puzzles or knowing devices of alienation; however abstract his discussions, he never abandons faith in the world of ordinary, basic feelings.

As a critic, Warner in all simplicity drew attention to this emotional character within work often thought of as dry and cerebral. 'Where allegory blends almost indistinguishably with reality there is the supreme achievement of art'; such a blend produces feelings 'more akin to wonder and delight than to the pleasure and excitement of intellectual understanding' (*The Cult of Power*, p. 65). The emergence, in the scene or the encounter, of something larger and richer than what is clearly apprehended, an emergence he always searched for and on occasions genuinely discovered, issues then in a kind of awe and joy – the obverse of the melancholy of deconstruction, that one be condemned to a world of perpetual glimpses of what one can never fully possess. Perhaps these alternatives also join in that continuous strife, which for Warner's favourite Heraclitus was the essence of justice; as Roy came to understand in respect of the Rector and the Air Vice-Marshal, 'between those two enemies there was something binding and eternally so' (*The Aerodrome*, p. 302).

Works by Rex Warner

The Kite, Blackwells, 1936.
Poems, Boriswood, 1937.
The Wild Goose Chase, Boriswood, 1937.
The Professor, Boriswood, 1938; Lawrence and Wishart, 1986.
The Aerodrome, John Lane, The Bodley Head, 1941; Oxford, 1982.
Why Was I Killed?, John Lane, The Bodley Head, 1943.
Poems and Contradictions, John Lane, The Bodley Head, 1945.
The Cult of Power, John Lane, The Bodley Head, 1946.
Men of Stones, John Lane, The Bodley Head, 1949.
Escapade, John Lane, The Bodley Head, 1953.
The Young Caesar, Collins, 1958.
Imperial Caesar, Collins, 1960.
Pericles the Athenian, Collins, 1963.
The Converts, The Bodley Head, 1967.

Index

Aerodrome, The   2–3, 5, 7–8, 15–17,
   19, 27, 36, 41, 50, 74, 75–111,
   112, 119, 123–4, 126–8, 135–6,
   148, 152, 155–6
Alcman   59–61, 71
Allegory 22–8
'Allegorical Method, The'   24, 28,
   106, 155
'Allegory, The Uses Of'   16, 50
Allen, Walter   17
Anaxagoras   138, 150
Athens, British Institute in   1, 125
Auden, W. H.   1, 6, 75, 81; 'Lay
   your sleeping head'   92; 'The
   Orators',   10, 35, 85; 'Paid on
   Both Sides'   7
Augustine   138, 151–2
Austria   14, 58

Battle of Britain   75
Benjamin, Walter   26, 27, 133
Bergonzi, Bernard   22, 31, 46
Birkin   39, 101
Blake, William   25, 119
Bond, Edward   73
Bowra, Maurice   7, 8
Brecht, Berthold   23, 56
Bunyan, John   2, 27, 38; The
   Pilgrim's Progress   13
Burgess, Anthony   20, 79, 82

Caudwell, Christopher   33, 145
Celan, Paul   135
Clifford, Gay   27, 37
Communism   12, 39
Conrad, Joseph   125, 132
Converts, The   3, 20, 124, 138–9,
   151–2
Crick, Joyce   17
Cult of Power, The   2, 113–14, 153

Dante   5, 24, 64
Day Lewis, Cecil   1, 7, 8, 10, 12,

38; The Buried Day   39; The
   Mind in Chains   12
Day-Lewis, Sean   21
de Man, Paul   25, 45
Dewey, John   78
Dickens, Charles   72
Dostoyevsky   17, 18, 44, 125, 128, 132
'Dostoyevsky and the Collapse of
   Liberalism'   17, 114, 153

'Education'   12
Enright, D. J.   17
Escapade, 18, 138

Fielding, Henry   56
Focus   16–17
Forster, E. M.   118
Fox, Ralph   118
Frankenstein   115
Fromm, Erich   78

Gadamer, Hans-Georg   25, 46
Gallic Wars   19
General Strike   7, 39
Graves, Robert 75; I Claudius 139
Gray, Thomas   100
Greene, Grahame   18
Guardian   76

Haggard, Rider   34
Hardy, Thomas   92
Hegel, G. W. F.   111
Heraclitus   119, 124, 156
Hill, Geoffrey   135
Hitler   58, 125, 139, 145
Homer   69, 71
Hopkins, G. M.   8, 36
Horstenau, Glaise von   58
Hoskins, Katharine   3, 51, 58
Housman, A. E.   63
Huxley, Aldous   12
Hynes, Samuel   3, 6, 13, 27, 35, 41,
   49, 52

158